Contemporary's
READER'S CHOICE
BOOK 2
CONNECTIONS

PEGGY A. GRIFFIN

Project Editor
Julie Landau

Project Associate Editor
Sarah Ann Schmidt

Consultant
Connie Spencer Ackerman
Consultant, Educational Services
Ohio Department of Education

Field-Test Coordinator
Ann Steiner
Chemeketa Community College
Salem, Oregon

Contemporary Books
CHICAGO

Photo credits
Page 1: AP/Wide World Photos. Page 9: Habitat for Humanity. Page 17: © John Running/Stock, Boston. Page 20: UPI/Bettmann Newsphotos. Page 25: Courtesy of the Mark Twain Museum. Page 28: The Granger Collection. Pages 33 and 36: AP/Wide World Photos. Page 41: UPI/Bettmann Newsphotos. Page 49: AP/Wide World Photos. Page 57: © Paul Damien/TSW-Click/Chicago. Page 65: © Peter Vandermark/Stock, Boston. Page 68: © Carla Hotvedt/Silver Image. Page 81: UPI/Bettmann Newsphotos. Page 84: Courtesy of N.O.A.A. Page 89: © Bruce Forrester/Jeroboam.

Cover photo © C. C. Cain Photography

This book is an educational textbook. Names, characters, organizations, places, and incidents on pages 9, 17, 49, 57, 65, 81, and 89 are used solely to illustrate the lessons contained herein and should not be considered real or factual. The persons portrayed in photographs on pages 9, 17, 20, 49, 56, 65, 68, 84, and 89 are models. Their actions, motivations, and dialogue are entirely fictional. Any resemblance to actual persons, living or dead, and actual events, locales, or organizations is entirely coincidental.

Copyright © 1992, 1989 by Contemporary Books, Inc.
All rights reserved

No part of this publication may be reproduced, stored in a retrieval system, or transmitted in any form or by any means, without the prior written permission of the publisher.

Published by Contemporary Books, Inc.
Two Prudential Plaza, Chicago, Illinois 60601-6790
Manufactured in the United States of America
International Standard Book Number: 0-8092-4426-8

Published simultaneously in Canada by
Fitzhenry & Whiteside
195 Allstate Parkway
Markham, Ontario L3R 4T8
Canada

Editorial Director
Caren Van Slyke

Editorial
Kathy Osmus
Craig Bolt
Sarah Conroy
Cathy Niemet
Robin O'Connor
Leah Mayes
Mary Banas

Editorial/Production Manager
Patricia Reid

Production Editor
Craig Bolt

Cover Design
Lois Koehler

Illustrators
Guy Wolek
Rosemary Morrissey-Herzberg

Photo Researcher
Julie Laffin

Art & Production
Princess Louise El
Carolyn Hopp
Andrea Haracz
Jan Geist

Typography
Terrence Alan Stone

Contents

Introduction v

PEOPLE

Lesson 1: An Unusual Teacher 1

Skill Build: The Five Ws ■ Finding Details Practice ■ The School Crisis ■ **Think It Through:** A Good Education? ■ Vocabulary Practice ■ **Word Attack:** Suffixes ■ **For Fun:** School Ethics

Lesson 2: Cora's New Home 9

Skill Build: Restating Ideas ■ Restating Practice ■ Low-Cost Housing ■ **Think It Through:** Who Pays for Housing? ■ Vocabulary Practice ■ **Word Attack:** More Suffixes ■ **For Fun:** Buying Property

Lesson 3: A Farmer's Day 17

Skill Build: Summarizing ■ Summarizing Practice ■ What Is Happening to the Family Farm? ■ **Think It Through:** How Did Farms Change? ■ Vocabulary Practice ■ **Word Attack:** More Suffixes ■ **For Fun:** Getting Around

ISSUES

Lesson 4: Mark Twain 25

Skill Build: Finding the Main Idea ■ Main Idea Practice ■ The Civil War ■ **Think It Through:** What Caused the War? ■ Vocabulary Practice ■ **Word Attack:** Prefixes ■ **For Fun:** Reading Maps

Lesson 5: Rosa Parks 33

Skill Build: Making an Inference ■ Inference Practice ■ A Decade of Civil Rights ■ **Think It Through:** What Are Civil Rights? ■ Vocabulary Practice ■ **Word Attack:** Prefixes That Mean "Not" ■ **For Fun:** Win Your Rights!

Lesson 6: An International Hero 41

Skill Build: Predicting ■ Predicting Practice ■ Puerto Rico ■ **Think It Through:** Puerto Rico: Some Facts ■ Vocabulary Practice ■ **Word Attack:** More Prefixes ■ **For Fun:** What's the Score?

WORK

Lesson 7: The Paycheck.....................49

Skill Build: Alike and Different ■ Comparison and Contrast Practice ■ What Happens to Your Paycheck? ■ **Think It Through:** Paycheck Deductions ■ Vocabulary Practice ■ **Word Attack:** Word Families ■ **For Fun:** Seeing Likenesses and Differences

Lesson 8: Job Clinic.....................57

Skill Build: Cause and Effect ■ Cause-and-Effect Practice ■ Work Attitudes ■ **Think It Through:** Good Work Behavior ■ Vocabulary Practice ■ **Word Attack:** Prefixes and Suffixes ■ **For Fun:** Writing a Memo

Lesson 9: Meggie Talks About Goals.....................65

Skill Build: Sequence Signal Words ■ Sequence Practice ■ Developing a Career ■ **Think It Through:** Setting Goals ■ Vocabulary Practice ■ **Word Attack:** Roots ■ **For Fun:** Picturing Your Ideal Job

SCIENCE

Lesson 10: Horoscopes.....................73

Skill Build: Find the Facts ■ Finding Facts Practice ■ The Constellations ■ **Think It Through:** Star Groups ■ Vocabulary Practice ■ **Word Attack:** More Roots ■ **For Fun:** Star Puzzle

Lesson 11: Diary of Janis Smith.....................81

Skill Build: Fact or Opinion? ■ Fact and Opinion Practice ■ Understanding the Weather Forecast ■ **Think It Through:** Weather Reports ■ Vocabulary Practice ■ **Word Attack:** Root Review ■ **For Fun:** Reading a Weather Map

Lesson 12: Community Recycling.....................89

Skill Build: Making a Hypothesis ■ Hypothesis Practice ■ America's Trash Problem ■ **Think It Through:** Why Recycle? ■ Vocabulary Practice ■ **Word Attack:** Review of Word Parts ■ **For Fun:** Recycler's Shopping List

Answer Key.....................97

Introduction

Welcome to *Connections*, the second book in Contemporary's *Reader's Choice* series. *Connections* explores issues that are important to everyday life—education, work attitudes, environmental awareness. This book gives you the information you need in today's world.

Connections will also help you understand and think about what you read. You'll learn tips for remembering what you read and ways to figure out the meaning of new words.

Each lesson contains the following parts:

- **High-interest reading** to introduce the lesson topic
- **Skill-building exercise** for understanding and practicing the reading skills
- **"One More Step"** to strengthen application of skills
- **Content reading** to give you background information on the lesson topic
- **"Think It Through"** to help you apply your skills
- **"Another Look"** to write about related topics
- **Vocabulary box** that can be folded back and held next to the content readings to define new terms
- **Vocabulary practice** to practice using new terms
- **Word-attack exercise** to learn vocabulary-building skills
- **"For Fun"** activities to read maps, charts, and other visuals

The books in Contemporary's *Reader's Choice* series are a bridge to reading whatever you want to read—newspapers, magazines, books, or information at work.

We hope you enjoy the lessons and activities in *Book 2: Connections*, and we wish you luck with your studies.

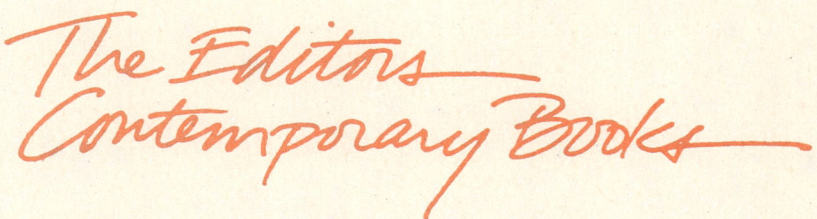

*The Editors
Contemporary Books*

PEOPLE

1 An Unusual Teacher

Stand and Deliver
★ ★ ★ ★
Starring Edward James Olmos
Directed by Ramon Menendez
Opens September 2 at the Fairfield Theater

A math teacher walks into his classroom holding an apple and a meat cleaver. His students look interested. He puts on a chef's hat and an apron, slowly raises the meat cleaver high into the air, and then chops the apple into two pieces. His students look stunned. Believe it or not, this is the beginning of a lesson on fractions.

There are many scenes like this in *Stand and Deliver*. This movie is about real-life teacher Jaime Escalante and his students at Garfield High School in East Los Angeles. Actor Edward James Olmos captures Escalante's passion and drive. The young actors who play students show how a school known for its drugs and gangs becomes famous for its big improvements in math.

Escalante sets rules for his students but also cares deeply about them. If he sees that a student is not listening, he playfully hits him with a red pillow. He tells students that they must have *ganas*, a Spanish word meaning "desire." He reminds them that they are the hope for the future.

Escalante also understands each student's special problems. In one scene, a student named Angel comes to see Escalante after class. Angel says that he wants to study at home, but he can't let members of his gang see him carrying books. So Escalante gives Angel two sets of books—one to keep at home and one to keep in his locker.

Some of the most moving scenes in the movie are based on actual events that took place in 1982. Escalante prepares his students to take a test in calculus, a difficult form of math. Officials are shocked when all 18 students, who come mostly from poor Hispanic families, pass the test. Accused of cheating, many of the students must retake the test. Again, they get high scores. Escalante complains that his students' scores were challenged only because the students are Hispanic.

You can't forget the faces and the stories of these students. This movie gets four stars, the highest rating.

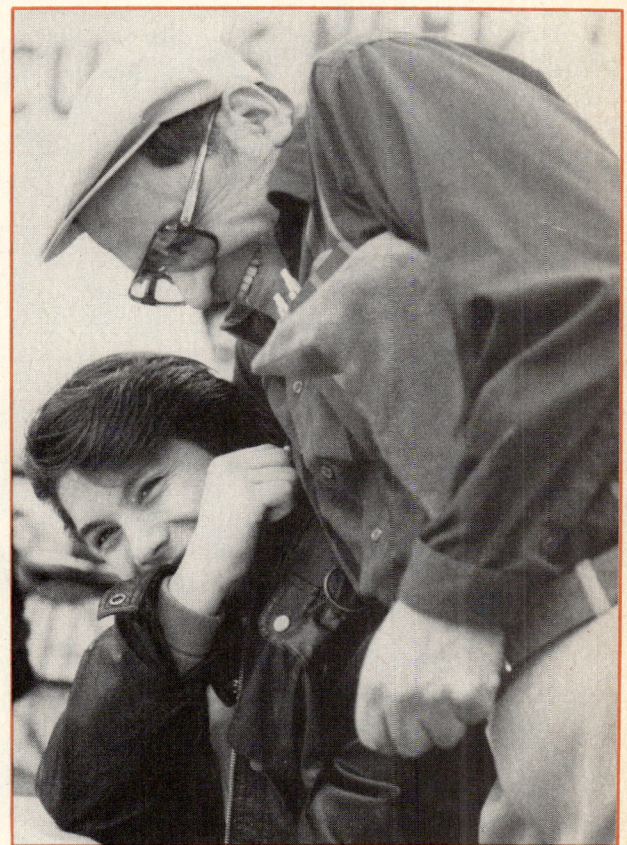

Jaime Escalante with one of his students.

SKILL BUILD

The Five Ws

A movie review gives you all the basic information you need. *Who* is the star of the movie? *What* is the movie called? *When* does it open? *Where* is it playing? *Why* should you go see it?

To understand anything you read, ask yourself these five W questions: *Who? What? When? Where?* and *Why?*

You can use this method to find details in any story or article. Try using the five Ws for the story you just read.

1. *Who* is the teacher? _____

2. *What* subject does he teach? _____

3. *When* does he take out a meat cleaver in class? _____
_____

4. *Where* is the school? _____

5. *Why* does the teacher hit students with a pillow? _____
_____

Your answers should be similar to these:

1. Jaime Escalante is the teacher.
2. He teaches math.
3. He takes out a cleaver at the beginning of a lesson on fractions.
4. The school is in East Los Angeles.
5. He does this to get students' attention.

▼ POINT TO REMEMBER

When you look for details in a story or article, always ask yourself the five W questions: *Who? What? When? Where?* and *Why?*

FINDING DETAILS PRACTICE

Directions: Read each story below. Then answer the detail questions that follow.

1. Maria James studied for a test the evening before it was to be given. That night, she dreamed that she had taken the test and gotten a perfect score. At 9:00 the next morning, her mother woke her and said, "Maria, you're going to be late for your test." Maria answered in a very sleepy voice, "I've already taken it."

    a. Who is the story about? _____
    b. What did she do on the evening before her test? _____
    c. When did her mother wake her? _____
    d. Where did the story take place? _____
    e. Why did Maria think she had taken the test? _____

2. Jules and Marta Zimmer both worked full-time. They never took vacations. But things changed when the teachers went on strike last September. The Zimmers used their vacation time to be with their children. They realized that they'd hardly spent any time with their children before. The family visited museums and parks together. They came to know each other better and grew closer.

    a. Who are the parents? _____
    b. What problem forced the Zimmers to use their vacation time? _____
    c. When was the strike? _____
    d. Where did the Zimmers go with their children? _____
    e. Why did they know their children better after the strike? _____

ONE MORE STEP

Think of the best or the worst experience you've had with a school. Then write answers to these questions.

Who was involved?
_____
_____

What happened?
_____
_____
_____
_____
_____

When did it happen?
_____
_____
_____

Where did it happen?
_____
_____
_____

Why did it happen?
_____
_____
_____
_____

The School Crisis

Since 1982, Jaime Escalante has repeated his success with his math students. This is just the **opposite** of reports on many other schools.

In 1987, the U.S. government came out with a **national** report card. The report compared student test scores in 1982 with recent scores. In almost half of the states, test scores had dropped.

Parents and teachers say that more money should be spent on the schools. But **administrators** point out that teacher **salaries** have gone up since 1982. The amount of money spent on each student has also risen. Increased spending alone has not brought higher test scores.

Another report shows that many high school graduates never did learn what they should have learned in school. Some graduates cannot subtract well enough to count change at the grocery store. Many people who hold **diplomas** cannot read or write very well. Both colleges and employers have complained about the poor skills of high school graduates.

Why do some students get such a poor **education**? Here are a few reasons that have been given.

• *Money* The national report shows an increase in teacher salaries. But this amount does not meet the rising cost of living. Teacher salaries are still low. More qualified people might take teaching jobs if they could be better paid.

Also, because of lack of funds, some students don't get the right books and materials. Some classes are too large, and teachers don't have time to work with each student.

• *The school system* Many teachers feel pressure to move students on to the next grade. Students are pushed ahead even if they don't understand what's going on in class.

• *Not enough involvement from parents* Studies show that much of a child's education comes from the home. Children tend to learn better when parents help with homework. But many parents lead busy lives. They don't take the time to encourage their children or find out how their children are doing in school. Other parents can't help out because the homework is hard for them, too.

What can be done about these problems? Groups of teachers and parents are working together to find **solutions**. Some **political** leaders are also trying to help. They are working to pass laws that will help teachers and students. ■

How can parents help their children succeed in school?

THINK IT THROUGH

A Good Education?

Part 1

Directions: Think about what you have just read. Then answer the questions below.

1. Who put out the national report on education? _____

2. When were national test scores higher—in 1982 or in 1987? _____

3. Who has complained about the poor skills of recent high school graduates? _____

4. Why are so few qualified people interested in teaching jobs? _____

5. What can parents do to help their children do better in school? _____

Part 2

Directions: Write answers to each question below.

1. Does a high school diploma alone mean that a person reads and writes well enough for college or work? Why or why not? _____

2. Why do some students get a poor education? List two reasons *not* mentioned in the article.

   a. _____
   b. _____

3. Name two groups that have organized to solve some of the problems in schools: _____ and _____

4. How can political leaders help solve problems in the schools? _____

ANOTHER LOOK

Think of a school that you know about. It could be a school you went to, the school your child attends (if you have children), or another school. Write a sentence naming *one* problem in that school. Then write a possible solution to that problem.

Problem: _____
_____
_____
_____

Solution: _____
_____
_____
_____
_____
_____
_____

VOCABULARY

administrators
people who run a school or school system

diploma
paper showing that a person has graduated from a school

education
learning

involvement
the act of taking part in something

national
having to do with the entire country

opposite
on the other side; as different as possible; for instance, *night* and *day* are opposites

political
having to do with government or a governing system

salaries
wages; pay

solutions
answers to problems

VOCABULARY PRACTICE

Directions: Write the answer that best completes each statement.

1. The students received _____ after completing high school.

    (a) computers
    (b) good grades
    (c) diplomas
    (d) thanks

2. They did not agree. Therefore, their views were _____.

    (a) political
    (b) encouraged
    (c) opposite
    (d) similar

3. Ms. Jones joined the local school council. She believes that her _____ will help her children.

    (a) salary
    (b) involvement
    (c) diploma
    (d) education

4. Teachers often strike for an increase in _____.

    (a) solutions
    (b) parent involvement
    (c) votes
    (d) salaries

5. Persons in charge of the school system are called _____.

    (a) principals
    (b) teachers
    (c) parents
    (d) administrators

6. A report on all of the schools in the U.S. is a _____ report.

    (a) large
    (b) national
    (c) local
    (d) good

WORD ATTACK

Suffixes

Many words are easier to read if you break them down into **syllables**, or beats. Say the word *thinker* and tap your finger each time you hear a beat. You should hear two beats in this word: think/er. Now say the word *diploma* and tap your finger with each beat. You should hear three syllables in this word: di/plo/ma.

Another way to break words down into smaller parts is to look for common endings, or **suffixes**. Take a moment to review these common endings:

Suffix	Meaning	Example
-er	one who	thinker
-ing	act of	thinking
-ly	in the manner of	softly
-est	most	highest
-ment	state of	achievement
-ness	in a state of	sadness

PRACTICE

Directions: Seven of the ten words below contain a suffix. Draw a circle around each suffix you find. Then, say each word aloud and listen to the number of syllables. Write the number of syllables on the blank line. The first one is done for you.

1. teach(er) 2
2. spending ____
3. school ____
4. learner ____
5. testing ____
6. highest ____
7. slowly ____
8. commitment ____
9. study ____
10. math ____

Teacher's Note: The focus in this book is on syllables as units of sound that students can hear and on the meanings of common suffixes and prefixes. For instruction and practice on the VC/CV and V/CV rules, see Contemporary's *Reader's Choice, Book 1: Insights* or Contemporary's *Critical Reading Skills* (pp. 50-54).

FOR FUN

School Ethics

People often have to make decisions based on their values. Read about the situations below. Then decide what each person should do and why. Write your personal opinion on the lines below.

1. Joe, a 17-year-old high school senior and football star, is trying for a college athletic scholarship. Joe and his teammates take steroids. Steroids are drugs that build muscles. One day Joe learns that some athletes have died as a result of taking steroids. However, he is afraid that if he stops using steroids, someone else will get that scholarship. What should Joe do, and why?

   _____
   _____
   _____
   _____

2. Margaret, a single parent, just moved to a new neighborhood. At her daughter's new school, the children say prayers every day. Margaret is not religious, and she objects to these daily prayers. However, she knows that most of the other parents support school prayer, and she doesn't want her new neighbors to dislike her. What should Margaret do, and why?

   _____
   _____
   _____
   _____

3. Rosa's son Billy has been doing poorly in his math class all year. Rosa meets with Billy's math teacher. The teacher confides that she plans to give Billy a high grade because she can't afford to have any failing students in her class. Then, Billy will have a high grade, but he won't have learned anything. What should Rosa do, and why?

   _____
   _____
   _____
   _____

2 Cora's New Home

Cora Jackson sat in the studio, tapping her toes nervously. She was waiting to appear on a TV talk show. The program began.

HOST: Good morning. This is "Meet the People," and I'm your host, Juan Winger. Today we will discuss Ownhome, a group that works with people to construct low-cost housing. Our guest is Cora Jackson, a woman who will soon move to a new home that she helped build. Welcome to the show, Cora.

CORA: Thank you. It's exciting to be here.

HOST: Cora, tell us about the apartment where you live now.

CORA: It's an old, run-down place. We have to keep patching up the holes in the wall, and we've never had indoor plumbing. It's small, too. My four children all sleep in one room. I had always dreamed of owning a nice house, but I couldn't afford to.

HOST: How did you learn about Ownhome?

CORA: My pastor told me about the program. He explained that Ownhome provides materials to build a house, and volunteers donate their labor. The family that will live in the house also works on it. After the family moves in, Ownhome can keep the payments low since they don't make any money on the deal. Anyhow, I knew I couldn't pass up this opportunity, so I went right out and put in an application. I'm thankful to have been chosen.

HOST: What was it like to help build your own home?

Volunteers at work on a new home.

CORA: I enjoyed it very much—and it was hard work! I was never the handywoman type. I pounded in a lot of crooked nails at first, but I've improved. And I have to hand it to my coworkers. They didn't look down their noses at me or treat me like a charity case. If they had, it would have been hard to accept this house.

HOST: Did your children take part in the project?

CORA: Yes. The younger ones didn't like it at first because they're shy and don't like talking to strangers. Janine, my eldest, loved it from the beginning. She's even talking about becoming a carpenter.

HOST: Any final comments on your experience with Ownhome?

CORA: I'd recommend the program to anyone. It changed my life.

HOST: Cora, thanks for sharing your story. We have to pause now for a message from our sponsor. We'll be right back with "Meet the People." ■

SKILL BUILD

Restating Ideas

- Cora has never had indoor plumbing.
- Cora has never lived in a house that had running water.

Both of these sentences say the same thing but in different words. The second sentence is a **restatement** of the first.

To **restate** is to say the same thing in different words. Try your hand at restating. Read the statement below, and then write a restatement of it.

Statement: Cora wasn't the handywoman type.

Restatement: _____

You could have written something like this: *Cora didn't have much experience in carpentry.*

Now try a different kind of exercise. Read the statements below. Match each statement on the left with its restatement on the right. Write the correct letter on the line.

____ 1. The 80-year-old house has fallen into disrepair.

____ 2. The house has been abandoned.

____ 3. The walls are collapsing.

____ 4. There is graffiti on one side.

(a) The structure is caving in.

(b) The old house in is bad shape.

(c) No one has lived there for a long time.

(d) Spray-painted symbols cover one of the outside walls.

Here are the correct answers: **1. (b)**; **2. (c)**; **3. (a)**; **4. (d)**.

▼
POINT TO REMEMBER

Restating is saying the same thing in different words. Practice restating what you read. You will find out whether or not you are really understanding.

RESTATING PRACTICE

Part 1
Directions: Match each statement on the left with its restatement on the right.

_____ 1. Construction of the new house begins in four days.

_____ 2. There is a nationwide effort to recruit help.

_____ 3. Community members are interested in the project.

_____ 4. The house will be completed in late spring.

_____ 5. A low-income family will occupy the house.

(a) Workers will come from all over the country.

(b) A low-income family will move in.

(c) We plan to finish by April or May.

(d) We will begin work within a week.

(e) The neighbors want to know more about the project.

Part 2
Directions: Read each statement below. Then write its restatement on the following line. The first one is done for you.

1. Brand-new houses can be expensive.
   It costs a lot to buy a brand-new house.

2. A house that was built more than 50 years ago may be a fire hazard.
   _____

3. The Tates borrowed money to purchase their house.
   _____

4. For the Rothmans, an apartment is more convenient than a house.
   _____

ONE MORE STEP

Ads in the real estate section of the paper can be hard to understand. Read the ad below and the restatements of information in the ad.

Apartment for rent
5 rooms;
   (*two bedrooms, living room, kitchen, dining room*)

near transportation;
   (*near bus and train*)

reasonable rent;
   (*$350 a month*)

utilities not included
   (*you pay for gas and electricity*)

Below is an ad for a house for sale. In your own words, restate what you think the advertisement really means.

House for sale
Charming starter home; cozy; convenient location; handyman's dream; make an offer

_____
_____
_____
_____
_____
_____

Low-Cost Housing

Like Cora Jackson, many Americans can't afford decent housing. Housing is said to be **affordable** if the rent or **mortgage payments** are less than one-third of the family's **income**. For instance, a single person who earns $1,050 a month should spend no more than $350 on housing. However, this amount is often not enough. Almost all of a family's income may go to housing costs, and their home may still not be fit to live in.

During the 1960s and 1970s, many people who could not afford housing lived in housing projects. These were funded by the **federal** government. During the 1980s and 1990s, the federal housing budget was cut. The federal government gave less and less money for housing. The burden shifted to state and local governments and small **nonprofit** groups. Now, the funding for low-cost housing comes from many sources.

Some groups, like Ownhome in the story, work mostly with **volunteers**. The volunteers build new homes or **renovate** old ones. The family that will live in the home takes part as well. After the family moves in, the payments are kept low. The group makes no profit.

Community development groups also provide low-cost housing. They work mostly with paid staff, not volunteers. These groups fix up old apartment buildings in a neighborhood, saving some buildings from being torn down. They offer the units to low-income people at a fair rent.

The community development group may be the landlord after the building is renovated. Often, the **tenants** in these buildings meet to discuss problems, so they have some control over the way the building is run.

Across the country, there are many groups working to solve the housing problem. Neighborhood banks have special loan programs. State and local governments give low-interest loans also. While all of these programs help create some new low-cost housing, many people say that it is not enough. They think that the federal government should pay for housing. ■

Why is it hard to find affordable housing?

THINK IT THROUGH

Who Pays for Housing?

Part 1
Directions: Circle the correct word or words to complete each sentence.

1. During the 1980s and 1990s, the federal government gave (*more/less*) money for housing.

2. The housing problem exists because people need homes that are more (*attractive/livable*).

3. Nonprofit groups (*knock down/repair*) housing that has decayed from lack of care.

Part 2
Directions: Read each statement below and write a restatement. The first one is done for you.

1. Statement: During the 1980s and 1990s, the federal housing budget was cut.

   Restatement: *The federal government spent less on housing during the 1980s and 1990s.*

2. Statement: The burden shifted to state and local governments

   Restatement: _____

3. Statement: Homelessness increased after federal funding was cut.

   Restatement: _____

4. Statement: Community development groups, neighborhood banks, and governments have formed partnerships to solve the housing problem.

   Restatement: _____

ANOTHER LOOK

Write an ad for the place where you live. On the top, write a description that would attract a renter or buyer. On the bottom, restate the description, telling just the facts.

Advertisement

_____
_____
_____
_____
_____
_____
_____
_____

Facts

_____
_____
_____
_____
_____
_____
_____
_____

VOCABULARY

affordable
sold at a price you can pay

community
neighborhood; area where one lives

developers
people who buy land and build houses at a profit

development
building or improving on property in a certain area

federal
national

income
money that you earn

mortgage payments
payments you make when you buy a house

nonprofit
not for profit or gain

profit
1. gain; 2. benefit

renovate
to make like new again

tenants
renters

volunteers
1. people who work without pay for a good cause; 2. to give without being asked

VOCABULARY PRACTICE

Part 1: Fill in the Blank

Directions: Fill in the blank with a word from the list below.

> profit renovate tenants income
> volunteers community
> mortgage payments developers

1. Lyle has a good job, but he spends most of his _____ on clothes.

2. The _____ met with their landlord to discuss the leaky roof.

3. The community group plans to _____ the old apartment.

4. The _____ spent 30 hours of their time putting up drywall.

5. The Jones family just moved to our _____.

6. _____ built a high-rise on the vacant lot.

7. If Stella misses too many _____, she may lose her house.

8. Chester is hoping to make a _____ in his new business.

Part 2: Multiple Meanings

Directions: Profit and *volunteer* both have more than one meaning. Decide which word correctly completes each sentence below.

> volunteer profit

1. We can't ask how old she is, but maybe she will _____ that information.

2. If Alberto can't make a _____, he will sell the store.

3. Listen to your sisters and brothers. You can _____ by their experience.

4. I need a _____ to help me paint the ceiling.

WORD ATTACK

More Suffixes

As you know, being able to recognize endings like *-ing* or *-ly* makes reading new words easier. Some endings can also help you understand what a word means. Take a look at the three words below. What does each word mean?

teach*er*: _____

work*er*: _____

homeown*er*: _____

A teacher is a person who teaches, and a worker is a person who works. A homeowner is a person who owns a house. What do each of these words have in common? _____
If you said that they all end in *-er*, you're right. The *-er* ending often means *a person who does something*.

Three other endings have this same meaning. They are *-or*, *-ant*, and *-ent*. Here are three examples:

visit*or*: a person who visits
occup*ant*: a person who occupies a house or apartment
resid*ent*: a person who resides, or lives, somewhere

PRACTICE

Directions: Imagine that you're helping to write a new dictionary. Write a short definition for each of the words below. Then pick two of the words and write a sentence using each one. The first one is done for you.

1. buyer: *a person who buys something*

2. renter: _____

3. actor: _____

4. accountant: _____

Now write sentences using two of the words:

Sentence 1: _____

Sentence 2: _____

FOR FUN

Buying Property

Even if you do have the funds to buy a house, the process can be tricky. Don't forget these important steps in buying a home.

1. To find the proper house or building, ask your friends if they know of a house for sale. You can also look at ads in the paper or go to a real estate agency. A real estate agent will charge a commission, or fee, for services.

2. When you find a house you like, have an expert (architect or engineer) make sure it's in good shape.

3. Make a deposit to hold the property.

4. Have a lawyer go over the contract, or sales agreement, carefully. The contract shows exactly what you are buying, and it states the terms of sale. If the contract looks fair, then sign it.

5. At the closing, or settlement, make your final payment. Then you will receive a deed that says that you are the owner of the property.

6. With mortgages, payments are very important. If you don't pay on time, the property may go into foreclosure. Then your bank or credit union can claim, or take back, the property.

TEST YOUR BUYING KNOWLEDGE

See how much you know about buying property. Match the sales terms in the first column with the definitions in the second column.

_____ 1. commission   **(a)** proof of ownership

_____ 2. deposit   **(b)** fee for agent

_____ 3. deed   **(c)** settlement

_____ 4. foreclosure   **(d)** claim on property if payments are not made

_____ 5. closing   **(e)** amount paid to hold property

3 A Farmer's Day

Chet Cranston watched TV as he had every day for the past month. It was only two in the afternoon, but already the sun was beating down through the living room windows that faced west. A pickup truck rumbled past the house, and clouds of dust rose from the road. Out the window, if you wanted to look (which Chet did not), you could see the acres of parched, dry ground that made up Chet's farm.

The phone rang, and Chet reached for it. "Hello?"

"Hey, Chet. It's Edgar." Edgar was Chet's youngest cousin. He had moved to the city ten years earlier. Chet got up and turned down the volume on the TV.

"It's good to hear from you, buddy! How are you doing?"

"Not bad, Chet. How's life on the farm?"

"To tell the truth, things aren't real good. I lost my whole crop this year. All of that good corn just withered up in the fields. It looks like we'll have to sell the place next year if we don't get some rain."

"Chet, I'm sorry to hear it. We heard about the drought on the news, but I didn't know you had it so bad."

"Edgar, this is so hard for us. The farm's been in our family for nearly 100 years. I was hoping that David would go on and take my place. But now . . . ." Chet's voice trailed off. Edgar had a good heart, but he couldn't know what this was like. Edgar liked living in the city. But Chet thought of himself as a farmer, and he couldn't imagine any other way of life.

"How's Lois? Is she there?"

"No, she's at work. She's a real trooper. She's been putting in 60-hour weeks at the store just so we can pay the bills."

"Chet, why don't the two of you come to the city for the weekend? You should relax and get your mind off the farm."

"Thanks, Edgar. It's kind of you to offer. Let me talk it over with Lois, and we'll let you know." Already, Chet's mind began to wander. Even if they sold the farm, they could keep the old house. They could lease some of the land, and Chet would still farm it.

"Well, Chet, it's been good talking to you."

"Same here, Edgar. Take care of yourself. You come visit us sometime."

"I'll do that. Good-bye, Chet."

"Good-bye."

Slowly, Chet put the telephone back in its cradle. He looked over at the TV but made no move to turn up the volume. He sat there, staring at the moving figures on the screen. ■

What is this farmer discussing?

SKILL BUILD

Summarizing

What if someone asked you to summarize quickly the conversation between Chet and Edgar on page 17? You wouldn't have time to tell all the details, like how long the farm had been in Chet's family and where Lois was working. Instead, you might say this: *Chet Cranston told his cousin Edgar that he might have to sell his farm.*

When you **summarize**, you put all the details together. Here's an example. Read these details.

   a. Last year, Chet's son David took the produce to market.
   b. Lois fed the chickens each morning.
   c. In the summer, Chet harvested corn.

How could you summarize the details? Here's one way: *Everyone in the family helped out with the chores.*

Now try it yourself. Read the details below and summarize them.

   a. Edgar sits at a desk all day at work.
   b. He takes the train home instead of walking.
   c. On the weekends, he watches football all day.

How would you sum up the details? _____

_____

You could have written: *Edgar doesn't get much exercise.*
   Try another one:

   a. Some families lose their farms because the crops fail.
   b. Some farms are lost because farmers go into debt.
   c. Other farms are lost because they are poorly managed.

How would you sum up the details? _____

_____

Here's one possible answer: *There are different reasons why families lose their farms.*

▼ POINT TO REMEMBER

To make a summary, ask yourself what the details have in common. Then put them together in one or two short statements. After you write a summary, check to see that it covers all the details.

SUMMARIZING PRACTICE

Directions: Read each list of details. Then write a one-sentence summary.

1. **a.** The ladybug and other beetles eat many insects that harm plants and animals.
   b. Some worms give air and fertilizer to the soil.
   c. Although people fear them, some snakes help farmers by eating rats and mice.

   Summary: _____

2. **a.** Grasshoppers have powerful hind legs and can make giant leaps.
   b. At times they go on distant flights.
   c. They destroy fields of plants for many miles around.

   Summary: _____

3. **a.** Our dog Shepherd knew each cow by name.
   b. When told to bring Bossie or Elsie, he brought that particular cow home.
   c. He sometimes went as far as three miles in the meadow to find them.

   Summary: _____

4. **a.** Farmhouses often have a rear entrance, since farmers come in from the fields with dirty clothes.
   b. Many farmhouses have offices.
   c. Because farm families were large, four-bedroom farmhouses are common.

   Summary: _____

5. **a.** The Brooklyn Bridge, completed in 1883, spans the East River from Brooklyn to Manhattan in New York City.
   b. It was the first bridge to use steel cable wire.
   c. It carries both automobile and pedestrian traffic.

   Summary: _____

ONE MORE STEP

Write some facts that you know about farms. These might be based on personal knowledge, TV news, a TV movie, or a motion picture.

Facts: _____
_____
_____
_____
_____
_____

Now write a summary sentence based on these facts.

Summary: _____
_____
_____
_____
_____
_____

What Is Happening to the Family Farm?

Over the past 100 years, America's farms have gone through many changes. At one time, farms were owned by families who lived and worked on them all of their lives. These families grew their own food. They also raised crops and animals to be sold. The farmers worked very hard, doing much of the work by hand.

Most farms were just large enough so that the work could be done by the family. On larger farms, some of the land wasn't used because of a lack of manpower. The land and the work were all in the family.

Farms changed as machines became cheap enough so that the **average** farmer could afford them. Farmers were able to work all of their land and more. Farms grew in size. Because the machines were so helpful, not all family members were needed to work on the farm. Children left to get jobs in towns and cities. The size of families became smaller. Family farms were changing.

Farmers were able to get more from each **acre** because of better seeds and **fertilizers**. They produced so much, however, that crop prices fell. Yet the costs of running a farm remained high. Many farmers were in trouble. The government tried to help by **subsidizing** farming. This included buying **surplus** grain and paying farmers not to farm certain acres. This only helped a little.

The government then offered loans to farmers. Farmers spent this money on more land and machines. Sometimes they spent too much and went into **debt**. Some farmers had poor crops because of bad weather or bugs. They lost money. Then the banks wanted the government loans paid back. Many farmers couldn't repay the loans and had to sell their farms.

The high cost of farming has caused some farmers to take second jobs. Others rent their land to other farmers. Some have sold their machines and taken different jobs. Other farmers sold some or all of their land to developers. **Developers** divide up the land and sell lots for houses or businesses.

The biggest change has been the **corporate farm**. This kind of farm is owned by a group of farmers or by a company. They hire workers and **managers** and run the farm as a business. This is a long way from the typical family farm.

Some independent farmers are still able to make a profit from their farms or at least break even. Every farmer dreams of doing well and keeping the farm in the family. Despite all of the changes in farming, many families are still holding on to that dream. ■

What difficulties lie ahead for this farmer?

THINK IT THROUGH

How Did Farms Change?

Directions: Check off whether the following statements are true (T) or false (F). Then explain your answer. The first one is done for you.

1. Farming has remained the same for the past 100 years. ☐ T ☒ F

   Explain your answer: *Farms have changed greatly because of machines, government loans, and corporate farming.*

2. A hundred years ago, most farm work was done by machine. ☐ T ☐ F

   Explain your answer: _____

3. Farm families are larger today than they were 100 years ago. ☐ T ☐ F

   Explain your answer: _____

4. Lower food prices will make more people start farming. ☐ T ☐ F

   Explain your answer: _____

5. In the future, corporate farms will become more and more common. ☐ T ☐ F

   Explain your answer: _____

ANOTHER LOOK

Holding on to the family farm is Chet's dream. What are your dreams? Write a few notes below and then write a paragraph about your dreams on another sheet of paper.

VOCABULARY

acre
a piece of land

average
common; normal; typical

corporate farm
farm owned by a group or business

debt
something you owe, usually money

develop
1. to buy land and divide it up for sale, usually with a house or a business on each lot; 2. to use chemicals to make a photograph visible; 3. to acquire gradually

fertilizer
something used to make the ground richer for plants

manage
1. to oversee workers; 2. to handle

subsidies
government aid based in money

subsidizing
giving subsidies, or grants of money

surplus
extra; more than enough

VOCABULARY PRACTICE

Part 1: Use Farming Terms

Directions: Fill in the blanks using the vocabulary words below. Sometimes two words are needed.

> debt   acres   subsidies   surplus
> average   developer
> corporate farm   fertilizer

1. We need to use _____ on our garden.

2. The national _____ is too high. The country spends more than it sells.

3. We have too many. What should we do with the _____?

4. His looks are just _____, nothing special.

5. All of these houses were built by the same _____.

6. The _____ turns farming into a business.

7. We bought one and a half _____ to build our house on.

8. The government tries to help farmers by using _____.

Part 2: Multiple Meanings

Directions: Develop and *manage* both have more than one meaning. Decide which word correctly completes each sentence below.

> develop   manage

1. Vernita works 50 hours a week, takes care of her children, and goes to night school. How does she _____ it all?

2. If you listen to a lot of music, you will _____ a good ear for it.

3. The photographer knew how to _____ the film.

4. My goal is to supervise, or _____, other workers.

WORD ATTACK

More Suffixes

- Karl was *hopeful* that he could save his farm.
- After the drought, Karl knew that saving his farm was *hopeless*.

In the first sentence above, the ending *-ful* tells you that Karl was *full of hope*. In the second sentence, the ending *-less* tells you that he was *without hope*. As with the ending *-er*, knowing suffixes such as *-ful* and *-less* can help you discover the meaning of a word that looks hard. Look at the chart below.

Suffix	Meaning	Example
-ful	full of	hopeful
-less	without	thankless
-ish	of, being	selfish
-able	of, being	agreeable

PRACTICE

Directions: Read the sentences below. Use the chart above to help you write the meaning of the **dark type** word.

1. George and Ruth love children, but they are **childless**.

    Meaning of word: _____

2. Isabella looks **boyish** even though she has long hair.

    Meaning of word: _____

3. It was an **eventful** summer on the farm. So many things happened!

    Meaning of word: _____

4. The tractor is still **usable** and will work for another year.

    Meaning of word: _____

FOR FUN
Getting Around

Directions: Jim Berendt lives on a farm just outside of Pearl City. The map below shows the area near his farm. Study the map, and then answer the questions that follow. Write your answers on another sheet of paper.

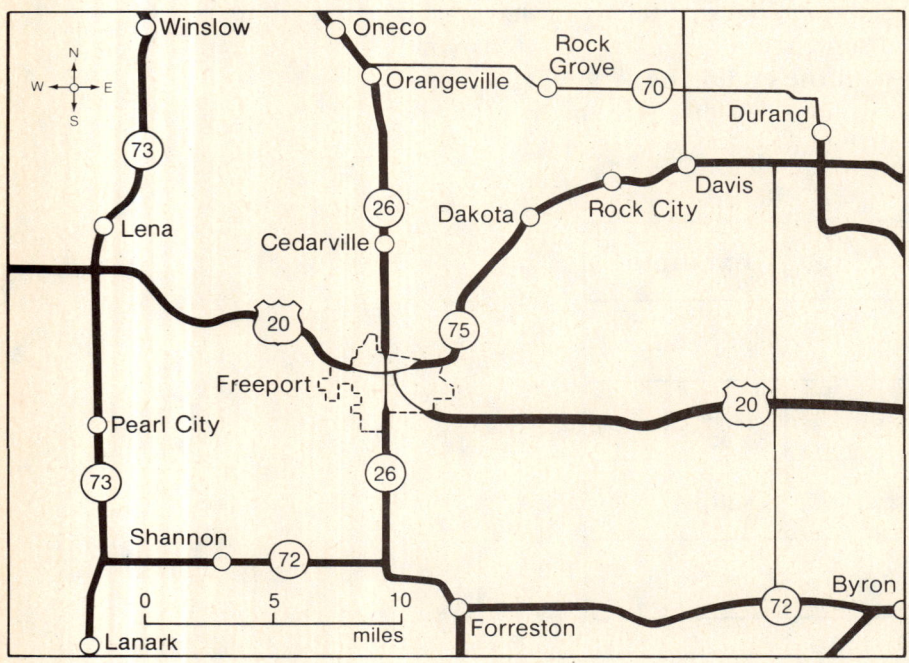

1. Where is the scale of miles on the map?

2. Find the compass on the map. Use the compass to tell if Freeport is east or west of Pearl City.

3. Jim plans to buy tractor parts at a store in Orangeville. He must first drive to Freeport. Should he go north or south when he leaves Freeport?

4. Each week, Jim and his wife go from Pearl City to Shannon to visit friends. About how many miles do they travel round-trip?

5. Jim's daughter lives in Davis and works in Byron. About how many miles does she travel on her way to work each morning?

6. Jim takes his produce to market from Pearl City to Freeport. By looking at the map, do you think the trip will be shorter if he takes Routes 73 to 20 or if he takes Routes 73 to 72 to 26?

4 Mark Twain

"At first I hated the school, but by-and-by I got so I could stand it."

"The widow said I was coming along slow but sure, and doing very satisfactory. She said she warn't ashamed of me."

The words above are lines from *The Adventures of Huckleberry Finn*. This novel and *The Adventures of Tom Sawyer* are familiar to most readers. Mark Twain is the author of both works. He has often been called one of America's greatest writers.

Mark Twain wrote before movies and television were invented. The wit and humor in Twain's books entertained people just like movies and television do today. Twain was also a famous public speaker. His words made people feel cheerful. Below are some examples of Twain's humor.

"Education consists mainly in what we have unlearned."

"When in doubt tell the truth."

"The man with the new idea is a Crank until his idea succeeds."

Mark Twain helped start a new trend in writing. He was one of the first writers to use the natural language of American people. The sentences from *Huckleberry Finn* at the top of this page are examples of this. The grammar isn't perfect, but the people sound real.

Most of Twain's stories tell about life in Hannibal, Missouri, where he spent his childhood. Twain was born to a poor family. His father died when he was 11. He left school to help his brother, who owned a newspaper. He began writing at an early age, using "Mark Twain" as a pen name. His real name was Samuel Clemens.

In 1870, Twain married Olivia Langdon. They had four children. Their home, in Hartford, Connecticut, was built to look like a Mississippi River steamboat.

Mark Twain died in 1910 at the age of 75. His writings have become even more well known after his death than they were during his life. ■

What kind of man was Mark Twain?

ISSUES

SKILL BUILD

Finding the Main Idea

In Mark Twain's autobiography, he wrote about his uncle's farm:

> It was a heavenly place for a boy, that farm of my Uncle John's. The house was a double log one, with a spacious floor (roofed in) connecting it with the kitchen. In the summer the table was set in the middle of that shady and breezy floor, and the sumptuous meals—well, it makes me cry to think of them.

What is the main idea of this paragraph, the main point that Twain is trying to make? It is that this farm was a wonderful place for a boy. The main idea is found in the first sentence. The other sentences are all **supporting details**. They tell why and how the farm was a heavenly place.

The relationship of a main idea to details can be compared to a building. The main idea is the roof. Details are beams, or posts, holding up the building. Each detail tells you more about the main idea.

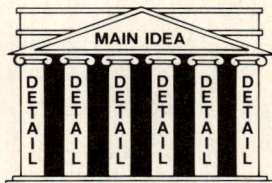

Where is the main idea found? It may be located anywhere in a passage, but it is often found in the first sentence.

Now try finding the main idea in the following passage:

> Mark Twain was known as a humorist. He was called this because he said many funny things. He was certain to make people laugh. His name was connected with humor.

The first sentence gives you the main idea. All the other sentences are supporting details. They tell why Twain was a humorist.

▼ POINT TO REMEMBER

The main idea is the point that the writer is trying to make. Details tell you more about the main idea.

MAIN IDEA PRACTICE

Directions: Read each paragraph below. Then list the main idea.

1. Samuel Clemens chose the pen name Mark Twain with care. From his days as a river pilot on the Mississippi River, Clemens remembered that the words "mark twain" were used to mean "safe water." The river pilots would call out these words when the water was deep enough for a boat to travel safely.

   Main idea: _____

2. Mark Twain paid his publishing debts by making speeches. He reworded sentences from his books to suit his audiences. He was famous for making speeches about his travels. During his lifetime, Mark Twain was more popular as a speaker than as a writer.

   Main idea: _____

3. Mark Twain once insulted another speaker by accident. He was scheduled to speak but was not able to appear. In his place was a speaker on the topic of temperance (anti-alcohol). Because Twain was known to be a witty speaker, the audience laughed at every word the gentleman said. They had mistaken him for Mark Twain.

   Main idea: _____

4. One of Twain's best-known novels is *The Adventures of Tom Sawyer*. Tom is always pulling pranks on his friends and relatives. In one part of the book, Tom's aunt asks him to whitewash a picket fence. Tom convinces his friends that painting the fence is an honor, not a chore, and he tricks them into doing it for him.

   Main idea: _____

5. *The Adventures of Huckleberry Finn* is about a young boy, Huck Finn, and a runaway slave named Jim. Huck and Jim travel down the Mississippi River together. They meet the different classes of people who live along the river. The character of Jim is based on a slave that Mark Twain knew in real life.

   Main idea: _____

ONE MORE STEP

The paragraph at the top of page 26 describes a place that Mark Twain remembered with great happiness. Think of a place that you remember fondly. Write some describing phrases to tell how the place looked or how it made you feel.

Place

_____
_____
_____

Description

_____
_____
_____
_____
_____
_____
_____
_____

The Civil War

When Mark Twain was growing up, **slavery** was accepted as a way of life. Slavery was a system in which people were owned like property and forced to work for other people without pay. They were not free. One of the main characters in Mark Twain's book *Huckleberry Finn* is a slave named Jim.

By the time Twain was an adult, many people did not accept slavery. The slaves themselves **rebelled**. They gathered in groups and rose up against their masters. If caught, they were **lynched**, or hung.

The slaves found sympathy from many white people who opposed slavery. These friends were called **abolitionists**. Abolitionists tried to end the slave system. They hid slaves and helped them escape to the North and Canada, where there was no slavery. They worked to change laws in the states that allowed slavery.

The United States became divided over the issue of slavery. Most Northern states **opposed**, or were against, slavery. Most Southern states **supported** slavery. The Southern states felt so strongly about keeping slavery that they **seceded**, or separated from the rest of the nation. They called their new nation the **Confederacy**. Their president was Jefferson Davis.

When the South seceded, the Northern states decided to call themselves the **Union**. Their president was Abraham Lincoln.

On April 12, 1861, Confederate soldiers attacked a Union fort called Fort Sumter, in South Carolina. This attack marked the start of the Civil War. At the beginning of the war, the South had better generals than the North did. However, the South had only 600,000 soldiers. The North had more men—almost three million (3,000,000) soldiers! Also, most of the factories and railroads were in the North.

For these reasons, the Union won the war. On April 9, 1865, the Confederacy's General Lee **surrendered** to Union forces.

During the war, in 1863, President Lincoln had signed the **Emancipation Proclamation**. This important **document** freed slaves in the South. After the war, Congress passed the Thirteenth Amendment to the Constitution. This law made slavery illegal everywhere in the United States.

The Civil War lasted four years and ended with two major results:

1. The states were again united. No state could secede from the Union.
2. Slavery was **abolished** in the United States. ■

Soldiers in a Civil War encampment.

THINK IT THROUGH

What Caused the War?

Part 1
Directions: Fill in the blanks with information from the reading.

1. The president of the Confederacy was _____.

2. The main issue that caused the war was _____.

3. Who was Abraham Lincoln? _____
_____

4. The document that freed many slaves was called the _____
_____.

5. Name two important results of the Civil War. _____
_____, and _____

Part 2
Directions: Use the time line below and the reading on page 28 to number the events in the order that they took place.

____ a. Slavery is ended by law in every state.
____ b. Fort Sumter is attacked, and the Civil War begins.
____ c. Southern states secede from the Union.
____ d. The Emancipation Proclamation is signed.
____ e. General Lee surrenders.

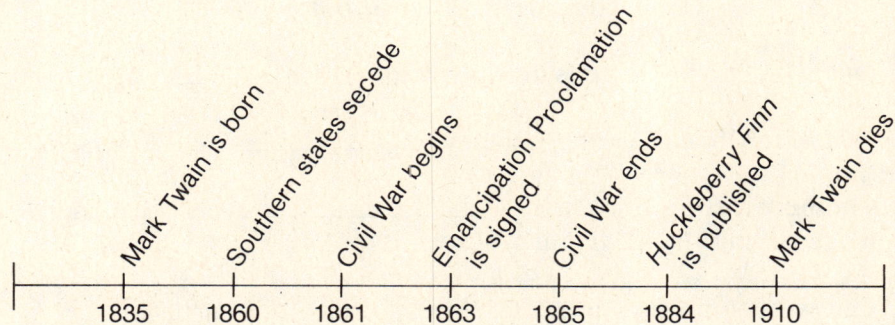

ANOTHER LOOK

The Civil War was fought more than 100 years ago. Its major effects on American society are still felt to this day.

Do you think that your life would be any different if the South had won the war? Write a paragraph explaining how your life would be the same or different. Then circle your main idea sentence.

VOCABULARY

abolitionists
people who worked to end slavery

Confederacy
Southern states during the Civil War

document
1. an official paper containing facts; 2. to give evidence of

Emancipation Proclamation
the document that freed slaves in the South

lynch
to kill by hanging

oppose
to disagree with

rebel
to rise up against, challenge

secede
to withdraw or separate

slavery
system in which people are owned like property

support
1. to be in favor of; 2. to pay the costs of

surrender
to give up, lose

Union
Northern states during the Civil War

VOCABULARY PRACTICE

Part 1: Work with Civil War Terms

Directions: Complete each sentence by filling in the blanks with a word from the list below. Sometimes two words are needed.

> slavery   Confederacy   oppose   Union
> surrendered   abolitionists   document
> Emancipation Proclamation

1. Do you support the new tax law, or do you _____ it?

2. The _____ worked to end slavery.

3. Because freedom is such an important right, it is hard to believe _____ was once a way of life.

4. The important _____ was used in court to prove the man's guilt.

5. President Lincoln signed the _____ even though some people wanted to keep the slave system.

6. The _____ lost the Civil War.

7. Lincoln was president of the _____.

8. Japan _____ to the United States at the end of World War II.

Part 2: Multiple Meanings

Directions: Document and *support* both have more than one meaning. Decide which word correctly completes each sentence below.

> document   support

1. One's birth certificate is an important _____.

2. Sasa barely makes enough money to _____ herself.

3. The new history book will _____ events that took place during the Civil War.

4. Can we count on your _____?

WORD ATTACK

Prefixes

• Lisa was **un**able to pass the test on the Civil War.

Many common **prefixes**, or word beginnings, have meanings. Knowing what these prefixes mean can help you understand new words without having to look them up in a dictionary.

The prefix *un-*, for example, means *not*. In the sentence above, you learn that Lisa was *un*able, or *not* able, to pass a test.

The chart below gives you several common prefixes and their meanings.

Prefix	Meaning	Example	Definition
un-	not	*un*able	*not* able
re-	again	*re*learn	to learn *again*
mis-	wrong	*mis*spelled	spelled *wrong*
anti-	against	*anti*war	*against* war
inter-	between	*inter*national	*between* nations

PRACTICE

Directions: Each of the words below contains a prefix from the chart above. Circle each prefix, then write the meaning of the word. Use the chart as a guide. The first one is done for you.

1. (inter)state   *between states*

2. antinuclear _____

3. mislead _____

4. unloved _____

5. rerun _____

6. unhappy _____

FOR FUN

Reading Maps

Map of the United States During the Civil War

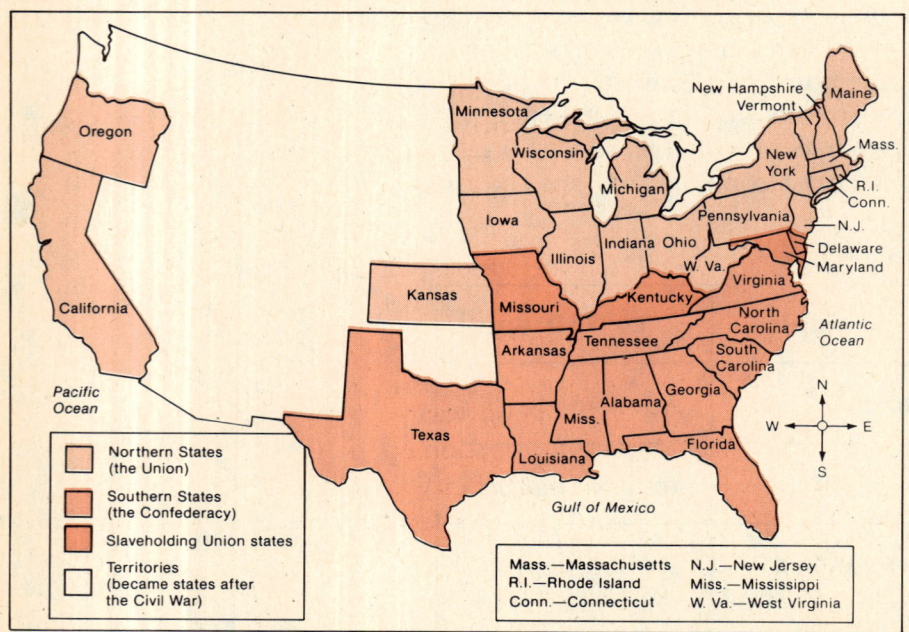

PRACTICE

Directions: Use the map to complete the exercise below.

1. Find the map key. Is the shading for the Union states lighter or darker than the shading for the Confederate states? _____

2. Name the two Western states that were in the Union. _____

3. Name the four slave-holding states that stayed in the Union. _____

4. Name five Confederate states. _____

5. How many states bordering the Atlantic Ocean were Confederate states? _____

5 Rosa Parks

December 1, 1955, marked a turning point in history. On that day in Montgomery, Alabama, a 42-year-old black woman named Rosa Parks finished a day's work. She was a seamstress in a department store. She picked up some items at a drugstore and walked to the bus stop. She waited in line, got on the bus, paid her fare, and took a seat in the front of the bus. By city law, blacks were required to sit in the rear of public buses. As more passengers boarded the bus, the driver asked her to stand and give her seat to a white man. Rosa Parks quietly said, "No."

The police were called, and Parks was arrested. She was bailed out of jail by E. D. Nixon, leader of the Alabama NAACP. Nixon and many other blacks formed a protest movement. Dr. Martin Luther King, Jr., then a young minister at a church in Montgomery, became the leader of this protest.

On December 5, 1955, the protesters began one of the most effective boycotts ever. They refused to ride the city buses. Of all the black people in Montgomery, 99 percent stopped riding buses. People walked to work or formed carpools. They said they were "walking for dignity."

The protest did not stop, though there were many hardships. For a year, black citizens of Montgomery stood up against arrests, bombings, and murders.

Rosa Parks was found guilty in court. Her case was taken to the U.S. Supreme Court. On November 13, 1956, the Supreme Court decided that Parks was right—bus segregation was wrong. Two months later, bus segregation ended in Montgomery and in every other city. Because of Rosa Parks's courage, people taking public transportation in the United States can sit wherever they choose. ■

Rosa Parks arriving to appear in court.

SKILL BUILD

Making an Inference

Rosa Parks was bailed out of jail by E. D. Nixon, leader of the Alabama NAACP.

From reading this sentence, what do you think is one function of the NAACP? _____

You're right if you said that the NAACP works to protect people's rights. But this is never directly stated in the story. You must **infer**, or put the clues together. In this case, your clues are:

- Rosa Parks was fighting for her right to sit on the bus.
- The NAACP supported her.

When you infer, you use details to make a guess about a message that is not directly stated. Try the next example. Read the sentence below, and then check off the inference that you can correctly make.

Dr. Martin Luther King, Jr., then a young minister at a church in Montgomery, became the leader of this protest.

Which inference can you make?

1. Dr. King had been a minister for a long time.
2. Church leaders sometimes take part in protests.

Did you choose **2**? Since Dr. King was a minister and he led the protest, you can safely guess that church leaders sometimes take part in protests. You could not infer choice **1** because the sentence says he was a young minister.

POINT TO REMEMBER

When you make an inference, you put details together to find a hidden message or suggested idea.

INFERENCE PRACTICE

Part 1

Directions: Read the following passages. After each passage are three statements. Place a check next to each sentence that is a correct inference based on the passage.

1. I once spoke briefly with Dr. Martin Luther King, Jr. I mentioned that I had met him in Boston several months before. He smiled and said, "Yes, you helped raise $160,000." I was amazed that in all of his travels, he could recall how much money a certain area had given.

   Which of these is a good inference based on the passage?

   _____ **(a)** Dr. King lived in Boston.

   _____ **(b)** Dr. King had a good memory.

   _____ **(c)** Dr. King was wealthy.

2. People who worked in the freedom movement knew that they might go to jail because of their beliefs. Those who had been to jail before spread the word on how to be prepared. Everyone in the freedom movement carried a toothbrush at all times.

   Which of these is a good inference based on the passage?

   _____ **(a)** Freedom movement workers were prepared to fight.

   _____ **(b)** There were thousands of workers in the freedom movement.

   _____ **(c)** Jails did not provide toothbrushes.

Part 2

Directions: What inferences can you make from this drawing?

ONE MORE STEP

After Rosa Parks was arrested, Dr. King made a speech in Montgomery. He said,

"For many years we have shown an amazing patience. We have sometimes given our white brothers the feeling that we liked the way we were being treated. But we come here tonight to be saved from that patience that makes us patient with anything less than freedom and justice."

From these words, what can you infer that Dr. King planned to do?

_____
_____
_____
_____
_____
_____
_____
_____
_____
_____

A Decade of Civil Rights

Rosa Parks's refusal to move to the back of the bus was not the first sign that people were unhappy with **discrimination** against blacks in the South. Discontent with **segregation** had been building for many years.

Southern blacks were unhappy with many conditions, including the following:

1. Most schools, eating places, rest rooms, hotels, and other **facilities** were segregated and displayed signs that read, "Whites Only." Blacks often traveled for miles without finding a place to eat, go to the washroom, or sleep.

2. Black people were forced to ride at the back of buses and trains even though they paid the same fare as whites did.

3. Registration tests and **poll taxes** kept most blacks from voting.

4. Many blacks were victims of lynchings and night raids on their homes by the Ku Klux Klan.

For these reasons, the civil rights movement gained strength in the years from 1955-1965. This **decade** was full of **protests** against all types of segregation. Groups staged "learn-ins" to support the right of black children to attend white schools. They organized "sit-ins" to give blacks the right to eat in all **restaurants**. At sit-ins, black and white people sat together at lunch counters. This was illegal. People **boycotted** businesses that did not hire blacks.

The largest of these **demonstrations** was in Washington, D.C., on August 28, 1963. At this demonstration, 250,000 Americans gathered in mass protest. Martin Luther King, Jr., gave his famous "I Have a Dream" speech.

Why is Martin Luther King, Jr., famous?

Two of the greatest **achievements** of the civil rights movement were the Civil Rights Act and the Voting Rights Bill.

The Civil Rights Act became law in 1964. It protects the rights of job hunters. According to this law, employers cannot choose whom they will hire on the basis of race, color, gender, religion, or nationality.

Before the Voting Rights Bill, some Southern states made people pay a fee, called a poll tax, before voting. If people had no money, they could not vote.

Some states also made people pass a test in order to vote. People who could not read well were prevented from voting since they could not pass the test. The Voting Rights Bill, passed in 1965, gave all people the right to vote by ending all voting taxes and tests. ■

THINK IT THROUGH

What Are Civil Rights?

Part 1
Directions: Answer the questions below in the spaces provided.

1. Name three results of the civil rights movement.

   a. _____
   b. _____
   c. _____

2. Does the Voting Rights Bill protect the voting rights of black people *only*? Explain. _____
_____

3. Does the Civil Rights Act protect the rights of women job seekers *only*? Explain. _____
_____

Part 2
Directions: Below are inferences you can make based on the reading. For each one, write a clue from the reading on page 36 that helps you make the inference. The first one is done for you.

1. The Ku Klux Klan is a terrorist group.

   Clue: *The Ku Klux Klan conducted lynchings and night raids.*

2. Historically, job discrimination has been a problem.

   Clue: _____
   _____

3. A "sit-in" is a peaceful protest.

   Clue: _____
   _____

4. Voter registration tests are now illegal.

   Clue: _____
   _____

ANOTHER LOOK

From the 1970s through the 1990s, people worked to improve the rights of disabled people. Many cities put ramps in shopping malls and on street corner curbs so people in wheelchairs could get around.

In 1973, the Rehabilitation Act was passed. This law says employers cannot discriminate against the disabled.

How is the movement in support of disabled people like the civil rights movement? _____
_____
_____
_____
_____
_____
_____
_____
_____

VOCABULARY

achievement
a goal that has been reached

boycott
a formal refusal to support a business or group

decade
a ten-year period

demonstration
the public display of a group's beliefs

discrimination
the treating of some people better than others without any fair reason

facilities
places that serve a particular function, such as rest rooms or drinking fountains

poll tax
a fee, now illegal, that had to be paid before a person could vote

protests
acts that show unwillingness to follow a course of action

restaurant
a public eating place

segregation
act of separating

VOCABULARY PRACTICE

Part 1: Fill in the Blanks
Directions: In the following paragraph, fill in the blank spaces with words from the list below.

decade   restaurant   facilities
protest   demonstrations

Civil rights have been won through much struggle. In the 1960s, people gathered in _____ to stage _____ against segregation. The years from 1955 to 1965 marked a _____ of civil rights activity. As a result, public _____ are now open to all races. All Americans have the right to sit in any bus seat or eat in any _____.

Part 2: Words Linked with Civil Rights
Directions: Circle each word that helped people get civil rights in the 1950s and 1960s.

1. lynchings
2. poll taxes
3. protests
4. segregation
5. demonstrations
6. discrimination

Part 3: Using Civil Rights Words
Directions: Write a sentence using each word pair.

1. discrimination—boycotts

   _____

2. segregation—achievement

   _____

WORD ATTACK

Prefixes That Mean "Not"

As you know, the prefix *un-* means *not*. If you are *un*happy, this means that you are *not* happy. Many other common prefixes also mean *not*. Take a look at the chart below.

Prefix	Example	Definition
in-	*in*correct	*not* correct
im-	*im*possible	*not* possible
non-	*non*smoker	*not* a smoker
il-	*il*legal	*not* legal
dis-	*dis*please	*not* please

PRACTICE

Directions: Each word on the left contains a prefix meaning *not*. Match each word with its definition on the right. The first one is done for you.

_C_ 1. uncertain

____ 2. insecure

____ 3. impatient

____ 4. disregard

____ 5. uncover

____ 6. discontent

(a) not patient

(b) to take off the cover

(c) not sure

(d) to not regard, not pay attention to

(e) not secure, not confident

(f) not content, not happy

39

FOR FUN

Win Your Rights!

Directions: Your goal in this game is to get 25 or more points. First, read all of the acts.

Acts

(a) The Civil Rights Act (1964)—protects against discrimination because of race, color, gender, religion, or nationality

(b) The Age Discrimination in Employment Act (1967)—makes sure that older people have an equal chance of being hired

(c) The Equal Pay Act (1963)—ensures equal pay for equal work

(d) The Rehabilitation Act (1973)—protects the rights of disabled persons

(e) None of these acts applies to this situation.

Now, read each case and decide which act would protect your rights. Fill in the letter of the act in the box. Check your answers and give yourself 5 points for each correct response. Did you get at least 25 points?

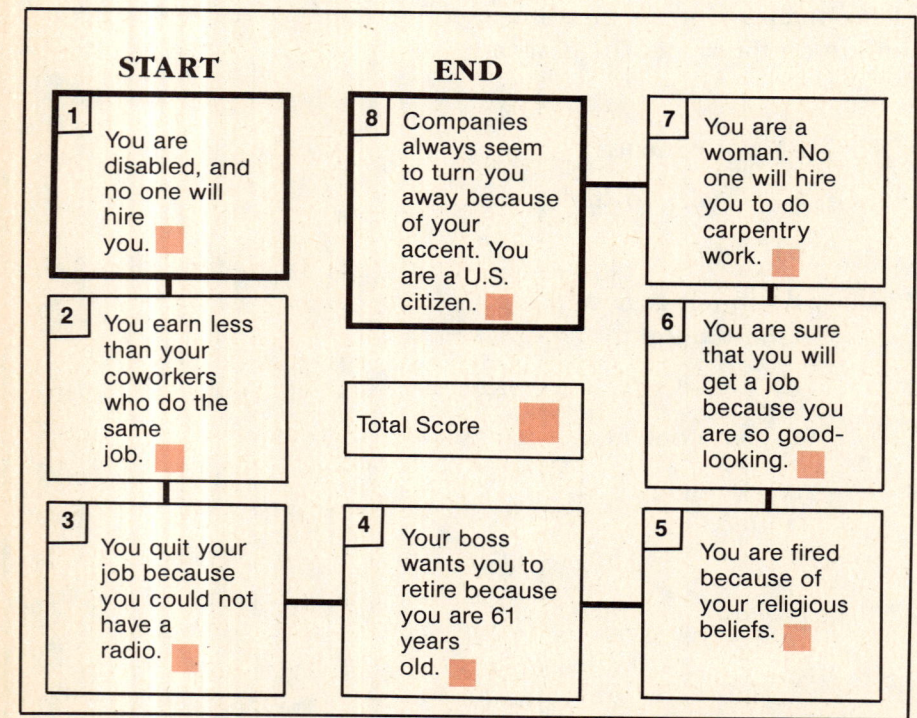

6 An International Hero

Name: Roberto Walker Clemente

Nickname: Bob

Birth date: August 18, 1934

Birthplace: Carolina, Puerto Rico

Last residence: Pittsburgh, Pennsylvania, and Rio Piedras, Puerto Rico (off-season)

Marital status: Married Vera Cristina Zabala. Three sons: Roberto, Jr., Luis, and Enrique

Height and weight: 5 feet 11 inches tall, 180 pounds

Profession: Baseball player

Beginnings: Softball player until age 17

Teams: Santurce Cangrejeros—1951-1953, Brooklyn Dodgers—1953-1954, Pittsburgh Pirates—1955-1972

Position: Right field

Outstanding characteristics: Could hit almost every kind of pitch, averaging over .300 in 13 seasons. Was a daring base runner. Threw out many base runners from his outfield position. Was called a "one-man team."

Highest batting average: .357 in 1967

Hits: 3,000

Runs batted in: 1,305

Home runs: 240

Injuries: Back and shoulder, bone chips, muscle pulls

Date of death: December 31, 1972. Clemente was on a mission to Nicaragua when he was killed in an airplane crash. He was delivering supplies that he had collected for earthquake victims there.

Honors: Elected to Baseball Hall of Fame in 1973. Voted National League's Most Valuable Player in 1966. Voted Most Valuable Player of 1971 World Series. Received 12 Golden Glove awards.

SKILL BUILD

Predicting

People were amazed at Roberto Clemente's fast movements. He could tell when a runner was headed for third base and could get him out with a swift throw. He could **predict** what his opponents were going to do. **Predicting** means looking ahead and guessing what will happen.

When you go to a ball game, you probably try to predict who is going to win. This is part of the fun of watching a game. You can also use this skill when you read. Good readers try to predict what the outcome of a story will be.

Try your predicting skills on the announcement that follows. Read it, then tell which statements are possible outcomes.

> The Heartmoor Club will be sponsoring its tenth annual softball tournament to benefit the Roseland Children's Hospital.

―――― **(a)** The game will raise money for the Roseland Children's hospital.

―――― **(b)** The tournament will be held in two years.

―――― **(c)** Children in the Roseland Children's Hospital will benefit from the tournament.

You should have chosen **(a)** and **(c)** as possible outcomes. The game is a benefit, so you can predict that it will raise money for the hospital. For the same reason, you can predict that children in the hospital will benefit from the tournament.

▼
POINT TO REMEMBER

Predicting means looking ahead. If you read carefully, you'll be able to predict the outcome of stories you read.

PREDICTING PRACTICE

Part 1

Directions: Read the advice that was given to Jack. Then choose the statement that tells what Jack will do *if* he follows the advice.

> "Good mental health is related to the willingness of a person to play, or be active."

_____ **(a)** Jack will take up a sport.

_____ **(b)** Jack will stop exercising.

_____ **(c)** Jack will work twenty more hours a week.

Part 2

Directions: Read each sports clipping below. Then check off the statements that are good predictions.

1. > The Redbirds' star player Ted Huntley limped off the field last night complaining of a pulled leg muscle. Without Huntley, the team doesn't stand a chance of winning Sunday's game against the Bluehawks.

   _____ **(a)** The Redbirds' winning streak will end.

   _____ **(b)** Huntley's career will end.

   _____ **(c)** Huntley will recover by tomorrow.

2. > For Phil Cragin of the Clinton State 49ers, homework is the name of the game. Cragin has been suspended from his college football team until he can maintain a B average.

   _____ **(a)** Cragin will be thrown out of school.

   _____ **(b)** College teams all over the United States will require better grades.

   _____ **(c)** Cragin will study harder.

ONE MORE STEP

Directions: Read the paragraph below. Then make a prediction about the future of baseball.

Roberto Clemente earned more than $100,000 a year. Just before he died, he was thinking about asking for $160,000. Today, the lowest salary in the big leagues is about $100,000. The highest is more than $6,000,000.

Your prediction about the future of baseball salaries: _____

_____
_____
_____
_____
_____
_____

Puerto Rico

Even though Roberto Clemente moved to the United States to live and work, he never forgot his native country, Puerto Rico. Before he died in 1972, Clemente was making plans to build a sports stadium for the young people of Puerto Rico.

Like Clemente, many Puerto Ricans come to live in the United States. About one-third of the Puerto Rican population live in the U.S. The largest Puerto Rican community is in New York City.

The Commonwealth of Puerto Rico, Estado Libre Asociado de Puerto Rico, is a **Caribbean island**. It is 110 miles long and 40 miles wide. Its shape is long and narrow, like a rectangle. The **population** is 3,670,000—more than 3½ million people.

The island's **climate** is warm and humid all year long. During the winter, Puerto Rico has a rainy season. This warm, **tropical** climate produces such trees as palms, hardwoods, bamboos, and mangroves. There are nonpoisonous snakes, lizards, mongooses, and many birds. Forty percent of the land is used for raising sheep and cattle. Pigs and poultry are also raised.

The leading crops are coffee, sugarcane, tobacco, and bananas. **Chemicals**, processed foods, machines, and metal products are made in factories. Most of these goods are sent to the United States.

The Taino Indians were among the first people to live in Puerto Rico. In 1493, Spain claimed the island. Many of the Taino Indians were killed by diseases spread by Spanish settlers. The Spanish brought slaves from Africa to do the work that the Indians had once done. Today, the population is a mixture of Spanish and African peoples. The main language is Spanish.

In 1898, Spain turned Puerto Rico over to U.S. forces. Since 1952 Puerto Rico has been a commonwealth. While it has a local government, Puerto Rico is still subject to many U.S. laws. Puerto Ricans are U.S. citizens and must serve in the U.S. military in time of war. They can elect local officials, but they cannot vote for U.S. president. They are represented by a non-voting member in the U.S. Congress. ■

THINK IT THROUGH

Puerto Rico: Some Facts

Directions: Imagine that you're helping to write an encyclopedia entry on Puerto Rico. Use information from page 44 to fill in the blanks.

Puerto Rico

Location: Puerto Rico is an island in the _____ 1 Sea. The capital city is _____ 2 .

Official language: _____ 3

Population: _____ 4

History: Some of the first people to live in Puerto Rico were the _____ 5 Indians. Spanish settlers claimed the island in _____ 6 . In _____ 7 , Spain turned Puerto Rico over to U.S. control. The island has been a commonwealth since _____ 8 . Puerto Ricans are U.S. _____ 9 , and they must obey many U.S. laws.

Climate: Puerto Rico's climate is _____ 10 and _____ 11 all year long. There is a _____ 12 season during the winter.

Agriculture: Animals raised include _____ 13 , _____ 14 , _____ 15 , and _____ 16 . Puerto Rico's most important crops are _____ 17 , _____ 18 , _____ 19 , and _____ 20 .

ANOTHER LOOK

Some people believe that Puerto Rico should become the fifty-first state in the United States. Others think Puerto Rico should become totally free and no longer be part of the United States.

What do you predict will happen to Puerto Rico? Which do you think would be better for Puerto Rico—to become a state or to become completely free? Why?

Prediction: _____
_____
_____
_____
_____
_____
_____
_____
_____

VOCABULARY

Caribbean
area including southern and eastern West Indies islands

chemicals
substances produced by science

climate
1. typical weather; 2. mood

island
land surrounded by water

population
number of people living in an area

territory
1. a part of the United States that is not a state and has its own government; 2. a geographical area belonging to or under the control of a government

tropical
hot and humid throughout the year; having to do with areas of the earth that are closest to the equator

VOCABULARY PRACTICE

Part 1: Work with New Words

Directions: Fill in each blank with the correct word from the list below. Use each word only once.

> island   chemicals   population
> tropical   independent   Caribbean

1. There is an _____ in the middle of the ocean.

2. He moved to a _____ climate for his health.

3. What is the _____ of your city?

4. Some farmers do not spray _____ on their crops.

5. Jamaica and Cuba are _____ islands.

Part 2: More Than One Meaning

Directions: Climate and *territory* both have more than one meaning. Decide which word correctly completes each sentence below.

> climate   territory

1. There was a _____ of fear after the war began.

2. The soldiers could tell that they had entered enemy _____.

3. Chicago's _____ is cold and snowy in winter.

4. Alaska was once a _____, not a state.

WORD ATTACK

More Prefixes

Some prefixes have meanings that tell when something will happen or when it *did* happen.

Suppose your teacher *postpones* a test. What does this mean? _____

You're right if you said your teacher delays the test. The test will be given *after* you thought it was going to be given. As you can tell, the prefix *post-* means *after*.

The chart below shows two prefixes that relate to time.

Prefix	Meaning	Example	Definition
pre-	before	*pre*paid	paid *before*
post-	after	*post*test	test given *after* something is completed

PRACTICE

Directions: Match each word on the left with its definition on the right. The first one is done for you.

_e_ 1. pre-Civil War   (a) *before* school

___ 2. postpone   (b) something shown or done *before* a flight

___ 3. postwar   (c) a test given *before*

___ 4. preflight   (d) to heat *before* cooking

___ 5. postmodern   (e) *before* the Civil War

___ 6. preschool   (f) to put off, delay until *after*

___ 7. preheat   (g) *after* a war

___ 8. pretest   (h) *after* the modern era

FOR FUN

What's the Score?

Directions: Read the information that is given about Roberto Clemente's statistics and study the abbreviation key. Then place the information in the chart below. Part of the chart is done for you.

Information:

The Pittsburgh Pirates drafted Clemente in 1954. That year he had two home runs, 38 hits, and 12 runs batted in. His batting average that year was .257.

In 1960, he helped the Pirates win the World Series. That year, he batted .314, hit 16 home runs, and batted in 94 runs.

In 1966, he hit .316 and had 29 home runs, the most for a single season in his career. He batted in 119 runs.

In his total career, he had 3,000 hits. He hit 240 home runs and batted in 1,305 runs. His career batting average was .317.

Abbreviation Key:

H—Hits
HR—Home Runs
RBI—Runs Batted In
BA—Batting Average

Roberto Clemente				
Year	H	HR	RBI	BA
1954	38	2	12	.257
1960	179			
1966	202			
Career Totals				

WORK

7 The Paycheck

Since he was a child in Bangkok, Thailand, Chai Boondee had dreamed of living in America. In school, he heard about people who went to the United States and became wealthy. He said to friends, "I want to start my own business. Going to the U.S. will be a way for me to do that."

Last year, at age 18, Chai came to the United States. After looking for a few weeks, he found work in a small restaurant. First, Chai was a dishwasher. Then he worked for two months as a waiter.

Joe, the other waiter, didn't talk much to Chai at first. Slowly, though, they became friends. Chai told Joe about his dream of becoming an American citizen and owning a business. Joe said, "Chai, I think you *will* do those things. You've picked up a lot of English in a short time, and our customers like you."

One night after work, Joe took Chai to a community college. Chai signed up for a business course and an English course. He was glad that the English class was free.

Then Chai was offered a job as a cook, and he eagerly took it. When Chai became a cook, he got a large raise. He worked hard and looked forward to his paycheck. However, he knew that some taxes would be taken out of the check since he was no longer on a tax-exempt work program.

Chai had heard about taxes in his business course, but he was still surprised on payday. Chai thought that his pay would be $200 a week, but his check was for only $139.98. After a talk with the restaurant owner, Chai understood more about taxes, unions, charitable contributions, and savings plans.

Several months later, Chai decided to join a union of restaurant workers and pay union dues each month. He also began giving $10 of each paycheck to a company charity fund.

To be sure that he saved some money, Chai joined a payroll savings plan. He knew he would need that money when he was ready to open his own restaurant.

What problems do restaurant workers face?

SKILL BUILD

Alike and Different

When Chai received his first paycheck as a cook, he did what most people do. He looked at it to see how much it was. The check looked just like he thought it would except for the amount of money he would take home. What Chai did is compare and contrast the check with what he thought it would be.

When you **compare**, you see how two things are *like* each other. When you **contrast**, you see how two things are *different* from each other.

Think about two of Chai's jobs at the restaurant. He worked as a waiter and as a cook. Write one sentence that *compares* the work of a waiter to the work of a cook, or tells how the two jobs are alike:

_____

_____

Your answer might be something like this: *Both a waiter and a cook talk to people all day.*

Now *contrast* these two jobs. Write a sentence that tells how they are different:

_____

_____

Here's a possible answer: *A waiter moves around, but a cook stays in one room.*

Try another example. Write one sentence that compares a restaurant to a supermarket. Then write a sentence that contrasts a restaurant with a supermarket.

Comparison (How is a restaurant *like* a supermarket?):

_____

Contrast (How is a restaurant *different* from a supermarket?):

_____

Were your answers like these?
Comparison: *Both restaurants and supermarkets sell food.*
Contrast: *You can get hot meals in a restaurant, but you usually can't get them in a supermarket.*

▼
POINT TO REMEMBER

To compare means to see how things are alike.
To contrast means to see how things are different.

COMPARISON AND CONTRAST PRACTICE

Part 1

Directions: Look at the outfits that were on display in a store window and read the statements that follow. If the statement tells how the outfits are alike, write *comparison*. If it tells how the outfits are different, write *contrast*. The first one is done for you.

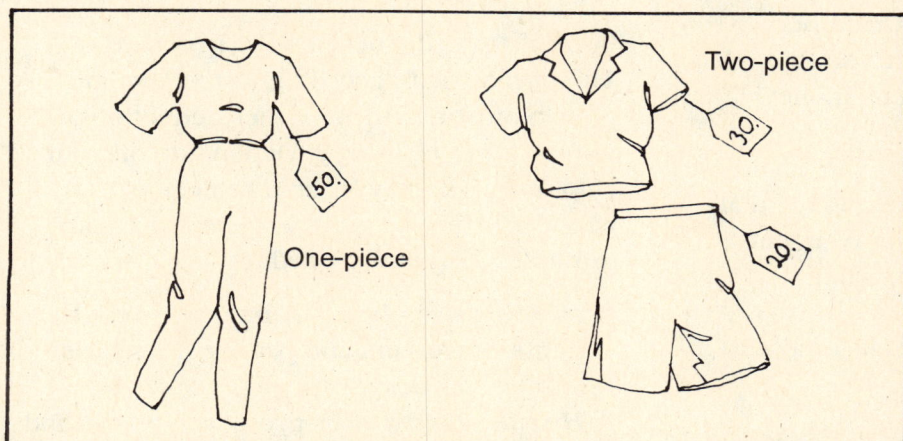

Comparison 1. Both are summer outfits.

_____ 2. One can be matched with other garments. The other can't.

_____ 3. The one-piece outfit is the same price as the two-piece.

_____ 4. The one-piece outfit is warmer than the two-piece.

Part 2

Directions: Read each sentence below and decide whether it compares or contrasts two things. Write either *comparison* or *contrast* on the blank line. The first one is done for you.

contrast 1. Freda has a new job that pays more money than her old job.

_____ 2. Freda is doing the same type of job that she did in her old company.

_____ 3. At her new job, she thinks it is harder to meet fellow workers than it was at the other place.

_____ 4. Both office buildings are on a city bus route.

ONE MORE STEP

Chai Boondee dreamed of owning a restaurant. What is your dream job? On the lines below, compare and contrast your dream job with work you have done in the past or with your current job.

Dream job: _____

Past or current job: _____

Comparison (How are the jobs alike?): _____

Contrast (How are they different?): _____

51

What Happens to Your Paycheck?

Like Chai Boondee, many people are surprised or upset by their first paycheck on a new job. It's never as much money as they expect. If you or someone in your family gets regular paychecks, you know that a person's take-home pay is only part of his salary. What happens to the rest of a worker's money? Where does it go?

The total amount of money you earn is called your **gross income**. The money that you actually take home is called your **net income**. The rest is taken from your paycheck in **deductions**. Below are two deductions taken from the checks of almost all American workers:

- *Income tax*—money taken by state and federal governments to be used for services such as education, public aid, and road construction. The amount of money taken ranges from 11% to 38%. This means that between 11 and 38 cents of each dollar is deducted.

- *FICA (Federal Insurance Contributions Act)*—money taken to give Social Security to people who are retired or no longer able to work.

Both of these deductions are **involuntary**. This means that according to the law, most people must pay them. Other deductions, though, are **voluntary**. Depending on your employer, you may be able to decide whether or not to pay them. Here are some examples of voluntary deductions:

- *Union dues*—help the union protect the rights of workers and pay for the salaries of union leaders.
- *Health insurance*—protects workers and their families against medical costs in case of an illness or accident.
- *Charitable contributions*—support good causes such as the Red Cross or United Way.
- *Payroll savings plans*—put money into a savings account for workers.

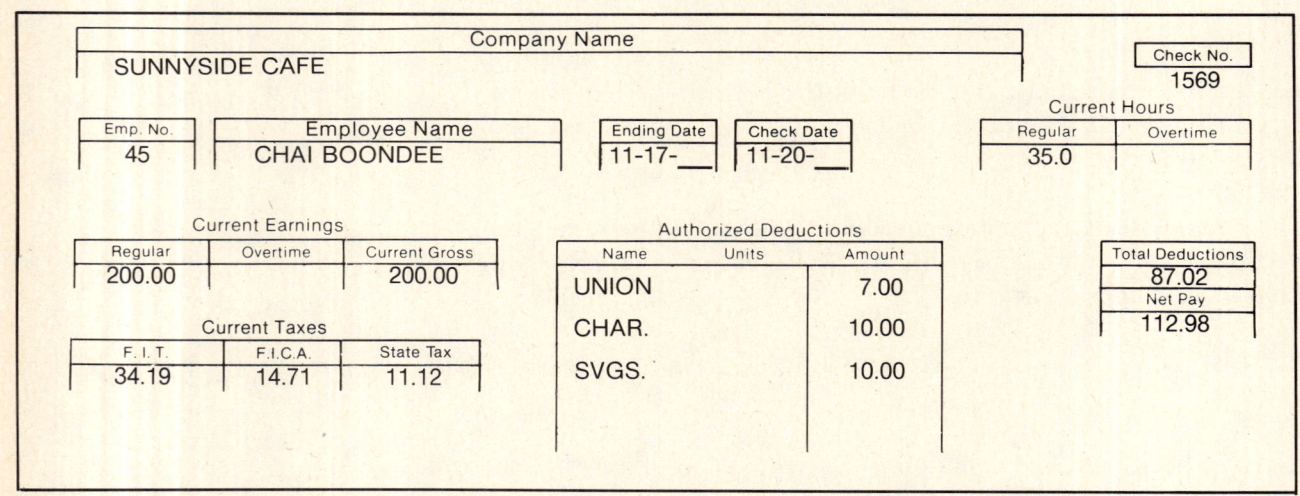

Is your paycheck similar to this one?

THINK IT THROUGH

Paycheck Deductions

Part 1

Directions: Check the correct answer, either true (T) or false (F).

1. All workers must join a savings plan.   ☐ T ☐ F

2. Gross income is income before taxes are taken out of a paycheck.   ☐ T ☐ F

3. Income tax is required by federal law.   ☐ T ☐ F

4. Fifty percent of each person's wages is taken in income tax.   ☐ T ☐ F

5. Most working citizens must pay income taxes.   ☐ T ☐ F

Part 2

Directions: Circle the answer that best completes each sentence.

1. Union dues can be used to
   - (a) give each worker a raise
   - (b) pay salaries of union leaders
   - (c) run the company

2. The new interstate highway will be funded by
   - (a) income taxes
   - (b) social security
   - (c) net income

3. When Kim's wife got sick, she was protected by Kim's
   - (a) payroll savings plan
   - (b) FICA
   - (c) health insurance

4. The shelter for battered women is funded by
   - (a) union dues
   - (b) social security
   - (c) charitable contributions

ANOTHER LOOK

Directions: Look at the deductions below. Each one is voluntary: you can decide whether or not to have it taken from your paycheck. Decide whether you would make each deduction below. Then tell why or why not.

1. Union dues
   Yes/No
   Why/why not? _____
   _____
   _____
   _____

2. Health insurance
   Yes/No
   Why/why not? _____
   _____
   _____
   _____

3. Charitable contributions
   Yes/No
   Why/why not? _____
   _____
   _____
   _____

4. Savings plan
   Yes/No
   Why/why not? _____
   _____
   _____
   _____

VOCABULARY

charitable contributions
money given to groups that help the needy, such as homeless people

deduction
money that is taken from your paycheck

FICA
social security

gross
a total amount; gross income is income *before* deductions

income tax
money used by the government to support public programs

insurance
protection against loss, damage, or illness

involuntary
not done or given with one's free will

net income
the amount of money that you have *after* deductions

union
a group of people who defend workers' interests

voluntary
something done or given with one's free will

VOCABULARY PRACTICE

Part 1: Choose the Right Term

Directions: Circle the correct word or words to complete each sentence.

1. The workers formed a (*FICA/union*) in order to get a raise.

2. Will your (*net/gross*) income be enough to buy a new coat?

3. (*Income tax/Net income*) is a worker's take-home pay.

4. Income tax is a (*charitable contribution/deduction*).

5. After Bill had the accident, he was glad he had (*insurance/FICA*).

6. Mary's grandmother is probably receiving (*social security/union dues*).

7. (*Gross/Charitable*) means total.

8. Our (*union/insurance*) charges dues.

Part 2: Complete the Paragraph

Directions: Place the words below in appropriate spaces in the passage that follows.

**income tax   involuntary   employees
social security**

For more than 100 years, U.S. citizens have had to pay _____. Over the years, these taxes have helped pay for national defense, new roads, better schools, and aid to farmers. In 1935, the U.S. government started FICA, or _____. This program gives assistance to elderly and retired people. Both of these deductions are _____. Most _____ must pay these taxes.

WORD ATTACK

Word Families

- Chai Boondee came to the U.S. **legally**. (legal + ly)
- In the U.S., drinking and driving is **illegal**. (il + legal)

As you know, adding prefixes and suffixes to a main word can change its meaning. In the **dark type** words above, the main word is *legal*. What is the suffix in the first word? _____ You're right if you said *-ly*. What is the prefix in the second word? _____ You're right if you said *il-*.

Both of these words are in the same word family. A **word family** is a group of words that share or come from the same main word. Below are a few words that belong to three different word families. The main word in each group is in **dark type** at the top of each column.

self	**love**	**friend**
selfish	lovely	friendly
selfishly	unlovely	friendship
selfless	lovable	unfriendly
unselfish	loving	friendless

Notice that these words are made simply by adding a prefix, a suffix, or both to a main word. The word *selfish*, for example, has a main word and a suffix: self + ish = *selfish*.

Now look at the word *unselfish*. It contains a prefix, a main word, *and* a suffix. Even though this word looks long, it's easy to break down into three small parts: un + self + ish = *unselfish*. How many syllables, or beats, are in *unselfish*? _____ You're right if you said three: un/self/ish.

PRACTICE

Directions: The words below come from the main word *think*. On the blank lines, write each word's prefix, or suffix, or both. Then write the number of syllables, or beats, in each word. The first one is done for you.

	Prefix	Suffix	Syllables
1. thinking	—	ing	2
2. unthinking			
3. thinker			
4. rethink			
5. unthinkable			

FOR FUN

Seeing Likenesses and Differences

Directions: Use your comparison and contrast skills! Study the word pairs in the left column. Then write words or phrases that tell how the word pairs are alike (comparison) and how they are different (contrast). The first one is done for you.

Word Pairs	Comparison	Contrast
1. office/ farm	Both are places to work.	Most offices are in cities. Farms are in the country.
2. waiter/ waitress		
3. paycheck/ cash		
4. citizen/ foreigner		
5. income tax/ health plan		
6. employer/ employee		
7. deduction/ raise		
8. Thailand/ United States		

8 Job Clinic

Dear Job Counselor:

I am a nurse's aide in a nursing home. We are always short of help. Even though I do the work of two people, my supervisor tells me I am too slow. She doesn't understand that I get tired.

I need this job because I have three small children. I don't want to go on public assistance. I am going to night school because I want a better job. It will take a long time for me to get a diploma because I can only take one class at a time. What should I do?

Signed,
Overworked in Oregon

Dear Overworked:

First, keep working hard in night school. A better education will be your ticket to a better job. Since you must work a while longer at the nursing home, you should stand up for your rights. Speak directly to the head of the nursing home. Use a positive approach by naming everything you like about the job. Explain why you want to work there. Discuss some of your goals. Offer some plans for a more realistic work schedule.

If this does not work, do not limit yourself to this one job. There are openings for hard-working, ambitious people like you. Good luck.

Dear Job Counselor:

I am a salesperson in a department store. I have been there for two years, and I like my job. I know how to take stock and handle customers in almost every department. My problem is that I want a raise, but I don't know how to ask for one. One woman was laid off after asking for a raise.

Signed,
Desperate for a Raise

What skills do nurses need?

Dear Desperate:

First, find out about store policies. What is the pay scale? Is there a union? After getting the facts, have a friendly talk with the department head. Mention your strengths as an employee, and say what you like about your job. Suggest ways that you can help the company grow. Your coworker probably wasn't fired just because she asked for a raise. Most likely, there were other reasons. If you use the right approach in asking for a raise, the worst that will be said is "No." Best of luck.

SKILL BUILD

Cause and Effect

In the letters you just read, both "Overworked" and "Desperate" are worried about complaining to their boss. They think their complaints might cause them to be fired. Both are afraid of a cause-and-effect relationship.

In a **cause-and-effect** relationship, one event makes another one happen. Here, the cause would be complaining to the boss. The effect might be getting fired.

Look at the words below. How often do you use them?

> because   therefore   since   for   so

These words are called **signal words** because they signal a cause-and-effect relationship. They tell you that one event has caused another one to happen. Look at the example below.

> Because she got a raise, Mary went out for dinner.

Because is the signal word. Getting a raise is the cause, and going out to dinner is the effect.

Now read the sentence below. See if you can find the signal word, the cause, and the effect.

> John worked overtime since he needed extra money.

Signal word: _____

Cause: _____

Effect: _____

Did you write these answers?
Signal word: *since*
Cause: *John needed extra money.*
Effect: *John worked overtime.*

Notice that either the cause or the effect can come first in a sentence. Order in a sentence does not change a cause-and-effect relationship. A cause *always* brings about an effect.

▼
POINT TO REMEMBER

Look for the signal words *because*, *therefore*, *so*, *since*, and *for*. They will help you find cause-and-effect relationships.

CAUSE-AND-EFFECT PRACTICE

Part 1

Directions: Read each sentence carefully. Are the words in *italics* the cause or the effect? Check the correct response. The first one is done for you.

1. Vera got a promotion *because she is a hard worker*. ☑ cause ☐ effect

2. *Phillip could not speak loudly*; therefore, he could not work as an announcer. ☐ cause ☐ effect

3. She worked at home *because it was easier*. ☐ cause ☐ effect

4. He was upset, *so he did not eat his lunch*. ☐ cause ☐ effect

5. Since Jerry had to work overtime, *he missed the party*. ☐ cause ☐ effect

6. Because Erica broke the machine, *the other workers wouldn't speak to her*. ☐ cause ☐ effect

7. *Helmut was sick for two days*, so he lost two days' worth of pay. ☐ cause ☐ effect

Part 2

Directions: Read each cause below, then write a possible effect. The first one is done for you.

1. Cause: Carol forgot to call in sick.
   Effect: *Her boss will be worried.*

2. Cause: Milton's boss rarely pays him on time.
   Effect: _____

3. Cause: Anita works very hard and doesn't set aside time to see friends.
   Effect: _____

4. Cause: Leonard thinks he is underpaid.
   Effect: _____

ONE MORE STEP

Directions: Carl has a hard time getting up for work in the morning. Think of two possible effects of this problem and write them below.

Possible effects:

1. _____

2. _____

Work Attitudes

Ask the average person why he works and he'll probably say, "To pay the bills." But is money the only reward people get from their work?

Though money is important, many people work for other reasons as well. In fact, many people **satisfy** deep personal needs through their work. Below are some reasons for working besides earning money:

1. *Being part of something important*—Many people take pride in working for a company that is making **advancements**.

2. *Being* **creative**—People like to solve problems and use talents that will improve the lives of others.

3. *Being part of a team*—Most people like to work with other people. Team spirit helps get a job done. When a team reaches a goal, each **individual** also reaches a goal.

Each of these reasons for working is important to a worker's job **performance**. A person is more likely to do a better job if he has a sense of purpose and a feeling of **accomplishment**.

Why are people fired from their jobs? In many cases, it's *not* because they are doing a bad job. Instead, people are often fired because of a personal conflict. This is why it is important to get along with fellow workers. Part of getting along with other people is a matter of good work habits. Here are tips for good on-the-job **behavior**:

1. **Promptness**—Getting to work on time and taking short breaks show you are **dependable**. People will know that you care about your work and coworkers.

2. **Courtesy**—It is easier to work with people who are pleasant. A good attitude helps create a good work **environment**.

3. **Eagerness**—Always work your hardest, even at a job that is not your first choice. Small jobs often lead to bigger opportunities. Your work record always follows you. ∎

Why is it important to develop good work habits?

THINK IT THROUGH

Good Work Behavior

Part 1

Directions: Do the following statements give correct information about the work world? Check true (T) or false (F).

1. All people work only to earn money. ☐ T ☐ F

2. Teams are only important in sports. ☐ T ☐ F

3. Most people leave jobs because the work is too hard. ☐ T ☐ F

4. The way employees act can affect a work environment. ☐ T ☐ F

5. Courtesy is important in keeping a job. ☐ T ☐ F

Part 2

Directions: Place a check next to each statement that relates to *good* on-the-job behavior.

_____ 1. The boss is out of town. Jim can leave early and no one will know.

_____ 2. May knew that her coworker was angry because of a personal problem. Instead of arguing, she decided to wait and discuss it later.

_____ 3. It was not required, but Harry learned to do more than just his job in the company.

_____ 4. Ann couldn't resist telling her coworker about the dance even though she was ringing up a sale at the cash register.

_____ 5. Tamara planned to quit her job. She gave two days' notice.

_____ 6. Isham stayed late to help a customer.

ANOTHER LOOK

Directions: Read the passage below, and imagine you are in this situation. Then answer the questions that follow. There are no right or wrong answers.

You are a data processor at Kirby, Inc. Ben, your best friend at work, has been late to work every day this week. His work is piling up, and the boss is starting to notice.

1. What could be *one* cause of Ben's problem? _____
_____
_____
_____
_____

2. How might Ben's problem affect *you*?
_____
_____
_____
_____
_____

VOCABULARY

accomplishment
a goal that has been reached; something completed successfully

advancements
improvements; movement to a higher rank or position

behavior
the way a person acts

courtesy
kindness, politeness

creative
imaginative; able to make new things and think of new ideas

dependable
reliable, worthy of trust

eagerness
interest; enthusiasm

environment
the people and things around you; your surroundings

individual
one person

performance
the way a person behaves on the job

promptness
the quality of being on time

satisfy
meet someone's needs or requirements

VOCABULARY PRACTICE

Part 1: Use Work Terms

Directions: Fill in each blank with a word from the list below.

behavior   accomplishment   promptness
creative   advancements
dependable   individual   courtesy

1. John was a _____ worker. He was always on time.

2. Finishing high school is a major _____.

3. _____ people look at the world in new ways.

4. Her _____ toward the client was rude and uncalled-for.

5. Always treat customers with _____.

6. They came to work on time because the boss demanded _____.

7. Modern _____ help people travel to work from long distances.

8. She would rather work in a group than as an _____.

Part 2: Choose the Right Word

Directions: Circle the word in parentheses ( ) that correctly completes each sentence.

1. Her (*eagerness/accomplishment*) during the interview got her the job.

2. A safe, clean work (*performance/environment*) is important.

3. As an artist, Fran uses her (*creative/dependable*) talents every day.

4. The way a person acts is called his (*behavior/advancement*).

WORD ATTACK

Prefixes and Suffixes

As you have learned, **word families** are groups of words that contain or come from the same main word. The words *legal*, *legally*, and *illegal* are in the same word family. The word *illegally* is also in this word family. What are the three parts in this word?

____ + _____ + ____ = illegally

Did you fill in the blanks this way?

il + legal + ly = illegally

Notice that *illegally* contains both a prefix and a suffix. How many syllables, or beats, are in this word? ____
You're right if you said four: il/le/gal/ly.

Take a moment now to review some common prefixes and suffixes and their meanings.

Prefix	Meaning	Example
un-	not	*un*able
non-	not	*non*union
im-	not	*im*possible
mis-	wrong	*mis*spelled
anti-	against	*anti*war

Suffix	Meaning	Example
-ful	full of	sin*ful*
-less	without	hope*less*
-able	able to	fix*able*

PRACTICE

Directions: On the lines below, write the prefix, the main word, and the suffix in each word. The first one is done for you.

	Prefix	Main Word	Suffix
1. nonsmoking	non	smoke	ing
2. misspelled	_____	_____	_____
3. unlikable	_____	_____	_____
4. unemployed	_____	_____	_____
5. disenchanted	_____	_____	_____

63

FOR FUN

Writing a Memo

Directions: Kevin Fisher is unhappy about changes in his job. Because Kevin has a hot temper, a friend at work told Kevin to write down his feelings before talking to the boss. Read Kevin's note below, then answer the questions that follow.

> Mr. Carter, I want to talk to you right now! What do you think you're doing? I don't like that cold, drafty place you have stuck me in. You don't pay enough for me to see the doctor if I get sick. You're nicer to the other workers than you are to me. If you don't move my desk back, I just might quit!

1. Think of two words that describe Kevin's note. _____

2. What do you think Mr. Carter would say or do if he read this note? _____

3. In the space below, write a new note for Kevin.

9 Meggie Talks About Goals

Good morning, students of Greer Business School. I am Mrs. Meggie Coles. It is a pleasure to talk to you today about reaching goals. I am a lucky woman because most of my dreams in life have come true. I always wanted to be in business for myself. Now I am.

I grew up poor but proud. My father worked in a steel mill. There were times when he was laid off from work. My mother paid our bills by doing domestic work. My parents taught my brother, my two sisters, and me to work hard. They also taught us to save and spend our money carefully.

My father often said, "The only way to get someplace in life is to go there yourself." By that he meant we should be independent and not count on other people to take care of us. I regret to say that he passed away when I was 13. Since I was the oldest, I dropped out of school at 15 to help my mother. Together, we did domestic work and took care of the younger ones.

After I was grown and married, I finished high school at night and completed two years of college. My husband and I opened a carpet cleaning business. It was natural for us to choose this business because we met doing home and office cleaning.

After a few years, our cleaning business grew into a carpet sales company. This was not easy for us, since we had not been trained in bookkeeping or accounting. Once, we almost lost our business because of our poor record keeping. We got in trouble with the Internal Revenue Service. We realized that we had to know more than how to clean and sell carpets, so we went back to school.

Just when my life felt complete with the business and our two wonderful children, things changed. My husband became ill. He lingered for two years and then died. Suddenly, I had to run a business and raise two children alone. As a woman, I had to struggle to gain respect in the business world. It was hard, but I did it.

I'm proud to tell you that my son and daughter are now running the business. I'm free to spend time with others, like all of you here today, who want to reach their goals. Thank you. ■

Like Ms. Coles, this woman is giving a speech.

SKILL BUILD

Sequence Signal Words

In her speech, Meggie Coles tells the story of her life. First, she describes her childhood, then she tells about her marriage and career. Finally, she describes her life today. Meggie describes her life in **sequence**, or in the order that events happened.

Everyday living is full of sequences. For example, most people eat meals in this order: breakfast, lunch, dinner. Getting up, going to work or school, then coming home is another daily sequence.

Reading passages also follow logical sequences. One way to tell the correct sequence of events in a passage is to look for signal words such as these:

> first   second   later   before   since   then
> last   after   when   next

Read the short passage below, and circle every signal word.

> Maverick's wife told him to take out the garbage, but he decided to do it later, after the football game. After the game, Maverick ate dessert. Then he washed dishes. Before going to bed, Maverick walked the dog. Last, he scrubbed the kitchen table. Maverick did everything—except take out the garbage.

Did you circle five signal words? *later*, *after*, *then*, *before*, and *last*.

Now read the sentences below. Number the events in the correct order. The first one is done for you.

____ Maverick walked the dog.

____ Maverick washed dishes.

____ Maverick scrubbed the kitchen table.

__1__ Maverick ate dessert.

You should have numbered the statements in this order: 3, 2, 4, 1.

▼

POINT TO REMEMBER

A sequence is a series—a number of events in order. Look for signal words to help you put events in sequence.

SEQUENCE PRACTICE

Part 1
Directions: Read Meggie Coles's speech on page 65. Then look at the pictures below. List them in the correct sequence.

a.

b.

c.

d.

Part 2
Directions: Read the story below, and circle every sequence signal word. Then place names of jobs on the time line by sequence.

Long ago, people worked with their hands. They gathered fruits and vegetables for food. Later, they learned to hunt and to prepare meat.

After settling together in communities, people began to farm. Next, some people became potters, tool makers, and carpenters.

Since then, many new areas of work have developed. Now people are employed in business, medicine, and social service positions.

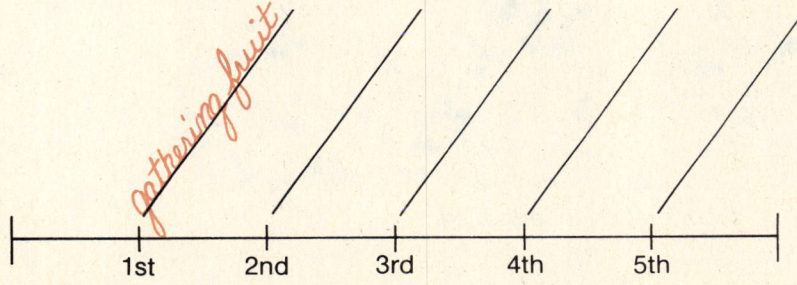

ONE MORE STEP

Directions: List in sequence three of the steps you will take to reach one of your goals in life.

Goal: _____
_____
_____
_____

Steps:

1. _____
   _____
   _____
   _____

2. _____
   _____
   _____

3. _____
   _____
   _____

Developing a Career

In the story you read, Meggie Coles went from cleaning houses to owning her own business. She used her talents to turn an ordinary job into something special. Meggie's **enterprise** can be a model for your own efforts in reaching goals.

Are you interested in developing your career? The list below will help you create a new role in life.

1. *Learn as much about your field as you can.* Read about your **occupation**. If there are newsletters or bulletins at work, read them. Daily newspapers can also be useful. Look in the "Business" or "Jobs" sections for articles about your field. Read the job **descriptions** in the want ads. Look for **announcements** about career **conferences**, or meetings. You can attend conferences to meet **experts** in various fields. You may also be able to get free information from the public library or from a local employment services office.

2. *Choose a role model.* Your role model will be someone who has done what you'd like to do. Find a person in your field whose work and **abilities** you admire. Spend time with this person, and ask what kinds of jobs the person has done. This will help you figure out how to get from where you are now to your dream job.

3. *Set goals.* Ask yourself these questions: "What is my career goal? What steps do I need to take in order to reach my goal?" Remember to reward yourself for steps that seem small, like reading an informative book or talking with someone about your occupation.

4. *Look at the problems you might face.* Ask yourself, "What **obstacles** will be in my way? How can I get around them?" Set **realistic** goals for yourself. If you need more education or training to advance your **career**, think about how you can get it. ■

How can this worker advance in his job?

THINK IT THROUGH

Setting Goals

Part 1: Work with Career Words
Directions: Fill in the blanks with information from the reading.

1. A _____ must be developed in steps.

2. One free source of information is the _____ _____.

3. Daily _____ carry announcements about jobs.

4. A person in your field whose abilities you admire can be a _____ _____.

5. At _____, you can meet experts in various fields.

Part 2: Choose the Right Word
Directions: Circle the correct word or words to complete the sentences below.

1. You may need more (*applications/information*) in order to set a goal.

2. All people (*can/cannot*) do all types of jobs.

3. The average person (*can/cannot*) become an expert in some area.

4. Most people (*do/do not*) have to overcome obstacles to reach a goal.

5. Seeing yourself in a new role is (*escaping from reality/an important step in reaching a goal*).

ANOTHER LOOK

Directions: Look through the want ads in your local newspaper. First find a job that suits your interests and abilities. Think about the steps you would take to get that position. Then, on the lines below, write three of the steps in sequence. Be sure to include any steps mentioned in the ad.

Position: _____
_____

Steps:

1. _____
_____
_____

2. _____
_____
_____

3. _____
_____
_____

VOCABULARY

ability
talent

announcements
public messages, often about events or meetings

aptitude
ability

career
life's work

conferences
gatherings at which people share ideas

description
details that tell what something is like

enterprise
business

experts
persons experienced in an area

obstacles
blocks; barriers; things that stand in the way

occupation
business; line of work

realistic
true to life

VOCABULARY PRACTICE

Part 1: Use Career Terms

Directions: Fill in the blanks with one of the words from the list below.

> occupation   descriptions   announcements
> experts   obstacles   realistic

1. Watch for _____ on the bulletin board.

2. Marge is _____ about her career goals.

3. Job _____ can help workers know what is expected of them.

4. Do not let _____ prevent you from reaching your goal.

5. The elderly men were _____ in wood carving.

6. Fixing cars is Larry's _____, or line of work.

Part 2: Work with Definitions

Directions: Match the definitions or examples on the right with the correct vocabulary word on the left.

_____ 1. occupation (a) notice
_____ 2. develop (b) waiter, baker, doctor
_____ 3. conference (c) lack of money, lack of time
_____ 4. enterprise (d) to plan to grow or change
_____ 5. obstacle (e) life's work
_____ 6. expert (f) seeing things as they really are
_____ 7. career (g) aptitude
_____ 8. ability (h) business
_____ 9. announcement (i) meeting
_____ 10. realistic (j) an authority in a field

WORD ATTACK

Roots

"Did Bud tell you the news over the **telephone**?"
"No, he sent me a **telegram**."

The words in **dark type** can't be broken into a prefix, main word, and suffix. If you break these words down, you'll find parts like *gram* and *tele*. These word parts are called **roots**. They come from the Greek language. Roots can't stand alone as main words do, but they have their own meanings.

Look at the chart below. It gives you five common Greek roots and their meanings. These roots will help you read and understand many new words.

Root	Meaning	Example
tele	far off, distant	telecast
phone, *phono*	voice, sound	telephone, phonotype
photo	light	photostat
gram, *graph*	written	telegram, autograph
scope	to watch, to look at	microscope

PRACTICE

Directions: Use the chart to figure out the meaning of the words below. Match each word on the left with its definition on the right.

_____ 1. *telescope*
_____ 2. *photocopy*
_____ 3. *photograph*
_____ 4. *telegraph*
_____ 5. *phonograph*

(a) *sound*, or music, *"written"* on a record

(b) a picture *"written"* on paper

(c) an instrument used to *look* at *distant* objects

(d) a *written* message sent from *far away*

(e) a copy of a printed page made using *light*

FOR FUN

Picturing Your Ideal Job

Most of us have complaints about our jobs. "The hours are too long." "The pay is too low." "My coworkers are unfriendly." These are just a few examples.

Think that these complaints are useless? Think again. Listing your gripes can help you discover what you really want in a job. To see how this works, try a simple exercise.

First, make a list of things you dislike about your job. Complain loud and long. Don't leave anything out!

Then, for each complaint, write a positive statement that tells about your ideal job. Some examples are shown below.

Complaint	Ideal Job
My job is boring and routine.	My job requires me to use my mind.
I work nights and have no social life.	I have reasonable daytime hours.
I have to travel an hour to get to work.	I work closer to home.

When you're finished, you'll have a picture of your ideal job. You may even find that you can get some of the changes you want at the job you have now.

10 Horoscopes

SCIENCE

General Outlook: You are very independent. You keep away from things that do not concern you, and some people may find you distant. You have a tendency to be shy. You have to make an effort to be social and not get overly involved in work.

You have strong opinions, although you do not always express them. Your sense of humor carries you through hard times. You have many dreams and fantasies. In the coming year, you can make some of your dreams come true.

Love: A solar eclipse will offer you the opportunity for a new love interest. Even though you are serious about your career, be open to the ways that this closeness can improve your life. Be willing to take risks even though you are cautious by nature.

Finances: Be very careful with money this year. Start a long-term savings program soon. April and May will be bad months for signing contracts. Someone may try to take advantage of you. In the fall, you may receive a bonus. The end of the year will be a good time to ask for a raise.

Career: You find satisfaction in your work, and you are ready to move up from where you are. This will be a good year to take classes and get more training in your field. You will have the patience to study and do research.

Health: You are in good health. Be sure to exercise and keep a good diet in order to stay that way. As you move up in your career, you will tend to neglect your body. Resist this temptation. Confiding in a close friend will ease stress.

Travel and Leisure: You will be invited to many parties. This will be a good year for you to take a winter vacation. Check your driver's license, insurance, and other papers. Be sure they are up to date if you plan to travel. ∎

♈	Aries (Mar. 21–Apr. 19)	♎	Libra (Sept. 23–Oct. 23)
♉	Taurus (April 20–May 20)	♏	Scorpio (Oct. 24–Nov. 21)
♊	Gemini (May 21–June 21)	♐	Sagittarius (Nov. 22–Dec. 21)
♋	Cancer (June 22–July 22)	♑	Capricorn (Dec. 22–Jan. 19)
♌	Leo (July 23–Aug. 22)	♒	Aquarius (Jan. 20–Feb. 18)
♍	Virgo (Aug. 23–Sept. 22)	♓	Pisces (Feb. 19–Mar. 20)

SKILL BUILD

Find the Facts

- Isabel's sign is Capricorn.
- Capricorn women are very thoughtful.

One of these statements is a fact, and the other is not. Which one is a fact? _____
You're right if you chose the first sentence. A **fact** is a statement that can be proved to be true. Anybody could prove that Isabel's sign is Capricorn by checking her date of birth. The second sentence is not a fact because it cannot be proved. We can't prove that all Capricorn women are thoughtful, and we can't all agree on what it means to be thoughtful.

Now try this example. Put a check by each statement that is a fact.

_____ 1. The sign of Leo is represented by a lion.

_____ 2. Reading your horoscope is the best way to plan your life.

_____ 3. People act strangely under a full moon.

_____ 4. A new moon occurs every 29½ days.

Did you choose statements **1** and **4**? These statements are facts because they can be proved. You can find the sign of Leo on a star chart. You can watch the sky to see how often there is a new moon.

Sentences 2 and 3, however, are not facts. We cannot prove that using a horoscope is the best way to plan one's life. Similarly, we all have different ideas about what is "strange." Even if we didn't, we still couldn't prove that all people act strangely when there is a full moon.

POINT TO REMEMBER

A fact can be proved to be true. Two ways to prove a fact are by seeing with your own eyes and by checking records.

FINDING FACTS PRACTICE

Part 1

Directions: Read each sentence below. Write *F* if the statement is a fact and *NF* if the statement is not a fact.

_____ 1. Space travel is a waste of money.

_____ 2. Scientists learn about the stars through space travel.

_____ 3. The North Star is the brightest star in the sky.

_____ 4. If you wish on the first star you see at night, your wish will come true.

_____ 5. Stars appear in the sky at night.

_____ 6. The Little Dipper is the most interesting star group.

_____ 7. The sun provides heat for the earth and causes plants to grow.

_____ 8. The earth is 92 million miles away from the sun.

Part 2

Directions: Below is a diagram of the star group Libra. Look at the diagram, and then check the statements that are facts. Note that some of the facts do not come from the diagram.

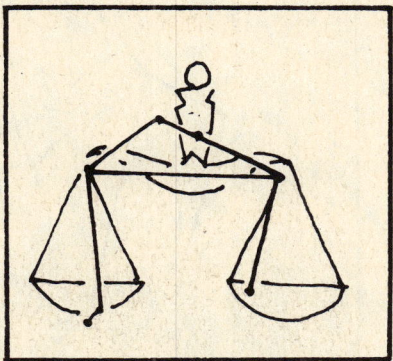

_____ 1. Libra is the only star group in the zodiac that does not represent an animal.

_____ 2. At one time, Libra was visible when the days and nights were equal in length.

_____ 3. People born under Libra are strong.

_____ 4. The stars of Libra can be drawn as a scale.

ONE MORE STEP

Directions: Write five facts about yourself. Then tell how each of them can be proved.

1. Fact: _____
_____

How to prove: _____
_____
_____
_____

2. Fact: _____
_____

How to prove: _____
_____
_____
_____

3. Fact: _____
_____

How to prove: _____
_____
_____
_____

4. Fact: _____
_____

How to prove: _____
_____
_____
_____

5. Fact: _____
_____

How to prove: _____
_____
_____
_____

The Constellations

What do Libra, Aries, Pisces, and Scorpio have in common? Of course, they're all signs of the **zodiac**. But you may not know that each one is also a constellation. **Constellations** are groups of stars that appear in a pattern. There are 88 known constellations.

Long ago, people noticed patterns or groups of stars. They imagined that certain star groups were shaped like animals, gods, and objects. To explain these shapes, they made up stories, now called **myths**.

An example is the myth about the constellation Gemini. According to the myth, these stars represent twins named Castor and Pollux who rescued shipwrecked sailors. Castor was a mortal, while Pollux was the son of a god. When Castor died, his brother refused to be separated from him, so the twins were placed together in the heavens. The stars in Gemini have nearly the same brightness, and they are closest together of all the stars in the northern sky.

Another group of stars is called the Northern Crown. According to the myth, the Greek god of wine married a princess and gave her a golden crown set with gems. When she died, he put it in the heavens. This star group is in the shape of a crown.

Of course, these myths can never be proved, and we no longer believe them. But the work of early astronomers formed a basis for modern **astronomy**. For instance, early astronomers drew maps that showed the place of each star group in the sky. Similar star maps are used today.

The constellations are still studied today. Astronomers use them to track the path of **satellites** sent into outer space. Sailors look at star groups to find directions when they are out at sea. And of course, ordinary people gaze at the stars.

Some people still believe in the practice of **astrology**. Astrologers predict the future based on the positions of the 12 star groups of the zodiac. They create star charts for people based on the position of the stars at the time of the person's birth. Another product of astrology is the **horoscope**. A horoscope is a daily prediction for each sign of the zodiac. While astrology dates back to ancient times, it has been **discredited** by modern science.

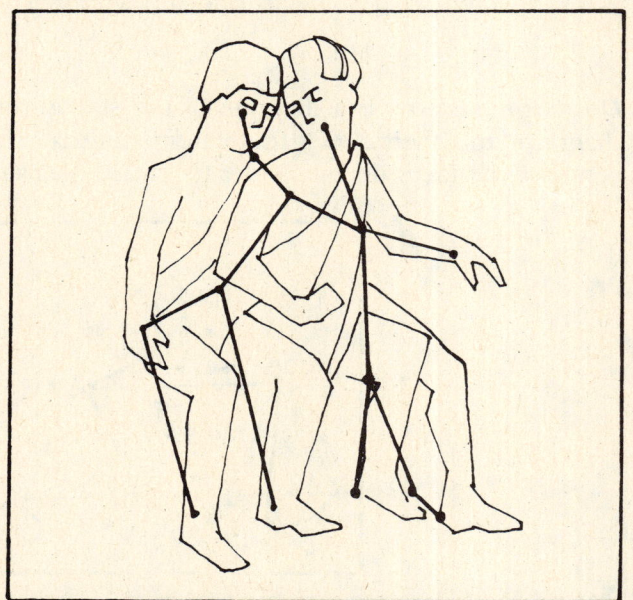

Castor and Pollux are the names of the twins in the constellation Gemini.

THINK IT THROUGH

Star Groups

Part 1

Directions: Circle the correct word or words to complete each sentence.

1. The study of constellations (*is*/*is not*) new.

2. A constellation is a group of (*stars*/*planets*).

3. Astrology (*is*/*is not*) accepted by scientists.

4. Castor and Pollux were (*seasons*/*twins*).

5. There are (*88*/*159*) known constellations.

Part 2

Directions: Write an answer to each question below.

1. Name three facts about the constellations:
   a. _____
   b. _____
   c. _____

2. Did early astronomers help advance the study of star groups? How? _____
_____

3. Why did people create myths long ago? _____
_____

4. What are some myths that people believe today? _____
_____

5. Do you believe in horoscopes? Why or why not? _____
_____

ANOTHER LOOK

Directions: Human beings may someday be able to live in outer space. If this happens, how do you think outer space should be used?

The list below gives some ideas. Choose one and complete the sentence that follows. Or think of your own use for outer space.
1. hospitals
2. waste dumps
3. prisons
4. food storage
5. farms
6. war zones
7. resorts

I would use outer space for _____ because _____
_____
_____
_____
_____
_____
_____
_____ .

77

VOCABULARY

ancient
relating to a time long past

astrology
the study of the supposed influences of the stars on human affairs

astronomy
the scientific study of the stars and planets

constellations
groups of stars forming patterns

discredit
to refuse to accept as true and correct

horoscope
prediction for each sign of the zodiac

myths
stories made up by early peoples

satellites
man-made vehicles that go around the earth or moon

zodiac
twelve constellations that form a belt which is the path of the planets around the sun; twelve symbols represent them

VOCABULARY PRACTICE

Part 1: Work with Astronomy Terms
Directions: Fill in the blanks with one of the words in **dark type**.

**zodiac   discredited   myths
constellations   ancient**

1. That old theory has been _____ by scientists.

2. The young child could not tell facts from _____.

3. There are 88 star groups called _____.

4. History books tell about _____ times.

5. Cancer is a sign in the _____.

Part 2: Match the Definitions
Directions: Match the vocabulary words in the column on the left with the correct set of examples on the right.

_____ 1. planets   **(a)** Gemini, Aries, Capricorn

_____ 2. myth   **(b)** 500 B.C.

_____ 3. zodiac   **(c)** Earth, Venus, Mars

_____ 4. ancient   **(d)** story about a goddess

Part 3: Using Star Terms
Directions: Write a sentence using each word pair.

1. astronomy—astrology

   _____

   _____

2. myths—constellations

   _____

   _____

WORD ATTACK

More Roots

The astronomer looked at the Big Dipper through her telescope.

You know what an astronomer does. What do you think the root *astro* means? _____

You're right if you said "stars."

As you have learned already, some words can't be divided neatly into prefix, main word, and suffix. You can't even break down the word *astronomer* into two roots! But knowing the root helps you guess the meaning. Below is a chart of more roots. Study the chart and do the exercise that follows.

Root	Meaning	Example
astro	stars; heavens; outer space	astronomy
bio	life	biology
meter	instrument for measuring	barometer
hydro	water	hydroplane
therm	heat	thermal
logy	study of	psychology

PRACTICE

Directions: Match each word on the left with its definition on the right.

____ 1. mytho*logy*

____ 2. *therm*ometer

____ 3. *hydrotherm*al

____ 4. *hydro*electric

____ 5. *astro*logy

____ 6. *bio*sphere

(a) relating to *hot water*

(b) electricity produced by *water* power

(c) the part of the world in which *life* can exist

(d) the *study of* how the *stars* affect humans

(e) *instrument that measures heat*

(f) *studies* relating to myths

FOR FUN

Star Puzzle

Directions: Look at the pictures of the constellations (or use your memory) to complete this puzzle. All of the answers are zodiac constellations.

Across
1. The water bearer
2. The fish
3. The bull
4. The scorpion
6. The scales of justice

Down
1. The ram
5. The crab
6. The lion

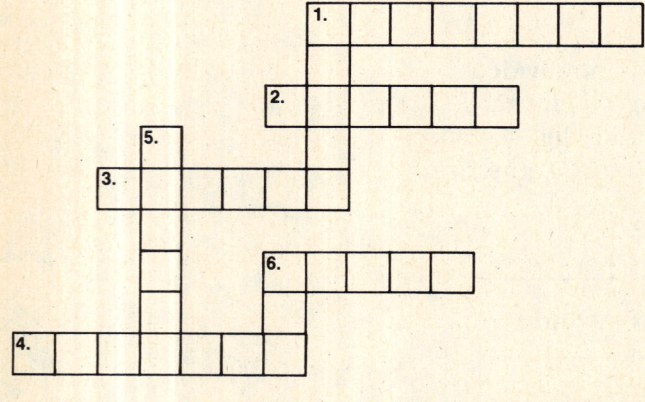

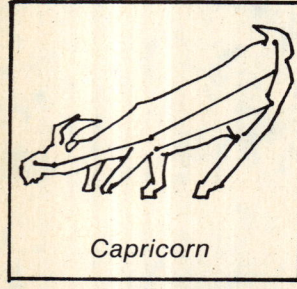
Capricorn

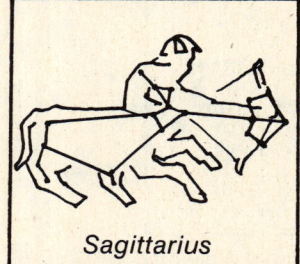
Sagittarius

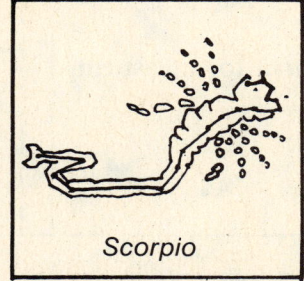
Scorpio

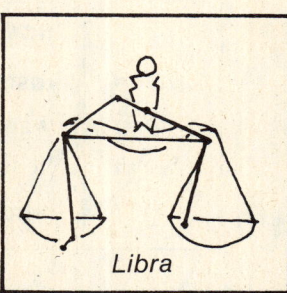
Libra

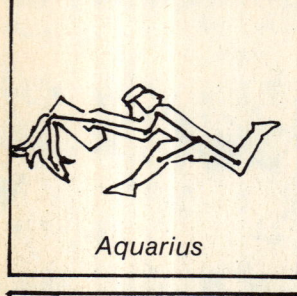
Aquarius

Leo

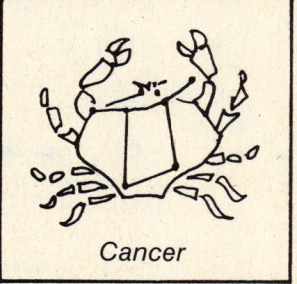
Cancer

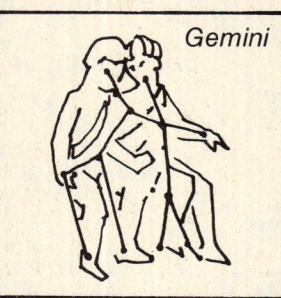
Gemini

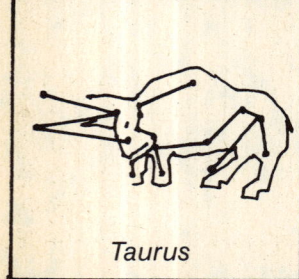
Taurus

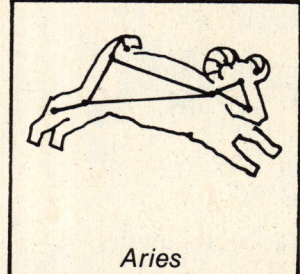
Aries

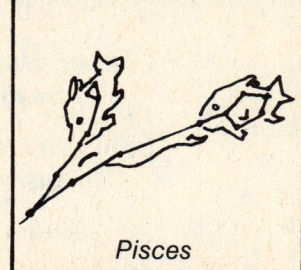
Pisces

Virgo

11 Diary of Janis Smith

In April 1965, more than 40 tornadoes swept through the Midwest. What follows are entries from the diary of a teenage girl who lived through this large-scale disaster.

April 11, 1965

Dear Diary,

Mom and Dad are begging me not to go to the dance tonight. They are worried about the 20 tornadoes that have struck in other states and the tornado watch that is out. Ralph will be here at seven, and I think I will go.

April 12, 1965

Dear Diary,

Ralph and I got back safely last night. I'm glad we didn't go out today, though. A tornado touched down here this afternoon at 4:05. I was listening to the radio when it happened. I heard my brother John calling me, and I ran out into the front yard. The sky was a deep greenish black, and off in the distance you could see a cone-shaped cloud.

The emergency sirens went off, and Mom sent us down into the basement. Rain began to fall, first in droplets and then in torrents. The wind got much louder. My ears still hurt from that awful noise. It was worse than the roaring of a hundred low-flying jets.

We heard tree branches slapping violently against the side of the house and the sound of breaking glass upstairs. Then lightning struck the house with a resounding crack. My brother John and I felt a small charge from it, and the whole house trembled.

When it seemed that the storm had passed, we made our way back upstairs. The living room windows had been shattered, and pieces of furniture were strewn across the room. Outside, a small tree lay across the driveway, uprooted by the storm.

April 13, 1965

Dear Diary,

We are still cleaning up our house. Dad says it will cost $10,000 to repair it. Ralph's family is fine, but their house was destroyed. They are staying with Ralph's uncle.

In the past two days, 47 tornadoes have hit the Midwest. They touched down in Iowa, Illinois, Indiana, Michigan, Wisconsin, and here in Ohio. The newspaper reported 257 deaths with $200 million worth of damage. This is probably the worst disaster I'll ever see in my entire life.

Mom is calling me. I have to go help with the work. ■

A tornado touches down in a farm community.

SKILL BUILD

Fact or Opinion?

On the night of April 11, Janis and her parents heard the same facts. They heard the Weather Service announce a tornado watch. After hearing this fact, though, Janis and her parents formed different opinions. The parents thought that it was better not to leave the house that night. Janis believed she would be safe.

You have already learned that a fact can be proved to be true. Now, what is an opinion? An **opinion** is a belief that cannot be proved. It is a personal judgment. Opinions depend on peoples' values and emotions. Everyone can agree on facts, but people do not always agree on opinions.

See if you can tell the difference between fact and opinion in the statements below. Write *F* for fact if the statement could be proved and *O* for opinion if it could not be proved.

_____ 1. Tornadoes are most common in the Central Plains states.

_____ 2. I think being in a tornado is a frightening experience.

_____ 3. Scientists are trying to learn how tornadoes are formed.

Compare your answers to these:

- Sentence 1 is a fact. You could prove it by checking weather records in all 50 states.

- Sentence 2 is an opinion because it depends on feelings. Most people are afraid of being in a tornado, but some might think it an adventure. In any case, there's no way to prove how people feel.

- Sentence 3 is a fact. You could check it by reading current scientific journals.

▼ POINT TO REMEMBER

A fact can be proved to be true. An opinion is a personal belief that cannot be proved to everyone's satisfaction.

FACT AND OPINION PRACTICE

Directions: Read the paragraphs below. Then indicate whether each sentence that follows is a fact or an opinion. Mark *F* and *O* in the spaces provided.

Paragraph 1

Many people claim to have seen balls of lightning. These strange fireballs seem to slide down fences, glide down hallways, and even pop through keyholes. Scientists are not sure that these balls exist. However, they keep records of sightings of the fireballs.

_____ 1. Reports have been made about seeing fireballs.

_____ 2. I believe reports of fireballs are false.

_____ 3. These reports are being kept on file.

_____ 4. Proof or no proof, the fireballs are real.

_____ 5. All these witnesses just can't be wrong.

Paragraph 2

It is difficult to measure the funnel of a tornado. These storms move fast and destroy almost everything in their path. Who wants to tangle with a tornado?

_____ 1. Scientists have difficulty measuring a tornado funnel.

_____ 2. Tornadoes move fast and do a lot of damage.

_____ 3. Measuring the funnel is a problem for scientists.

_____ 4. The study of tornadoes is a waste of time.

_____ 5. If you measure one, you will become famous.

ONE MORE STEP

Directions: Read the advertisement below. Then write one sentence that states a fact about this advertisement and a sentence that states your own opinion of it.

> Protect your family with Zebrow Insurance. You can be sure that Zebrow offers the best plan for tornado and flood damage. Checks and credit cards are accepted.
>
> **Z**ebrow
> *The Safe Home Company*

Fact: _____

_____

Your opinion: _____

_____
_____
_____
_____

Understanding the Weather Forecast

Janis and her parents probably would have been helped by a better understanding of weather **forecasts**. For example, did they know the difference between a tornado watch and a tornado warning? During a watch, conditions are ideal for a tornado. A warning means that a tornado has been sighted in the area and may touch down.

Perhaps you have decided to go swimming or cancel a picnic based on weather **predictions**. **Meteorologists** do not claim to be right all the time, but they can give you some helpful information.

The terms below are used in many local forecasts.

- *Average temperature*—an average of the **temperature** readings taken hourly for twenty-four hours.

- *Relative humidity*—the percentage of moisture in the air morning, noon, and evening. Some sample readings: 6 A.M., 73 percent; noon, 58 percent; 6 P.M., 67 percent. When it's raining, relative humidity is 100 percent.

- *Precipitation*—a report on the amount of moisture falling to earth in the form of rain, snow, hail, or sleet.

- *Highest wind velocity*—greatest wind speed. On a mild day, winds would be 10 mph (miles per hour). High winds are 50-60 mph. Low winds are 0-5 mph.

- *Barometric pressure*—readings from a **barometer**, a device that records air pressure. Thirty is a normal reading; 29.5 is low; 30.5 is high.

- *Windchill factor*—measures how much colder wind makes the air feel. For example, a recorded temperature of 5 degrees with a 45 mph wind has a chill factor of 46 degrees below zero.

Certain words used in weather reports can alert you to weather changes. For instance, rain is likely when you hear these words: humid, high barometric pressure, or precipitation. When you hear that a warm front is coming to a cold area, be prepared for snow, because snow is formed when warm and cold air mix in the clouds. Falling temperatures may mean that a freeze is coming. ■

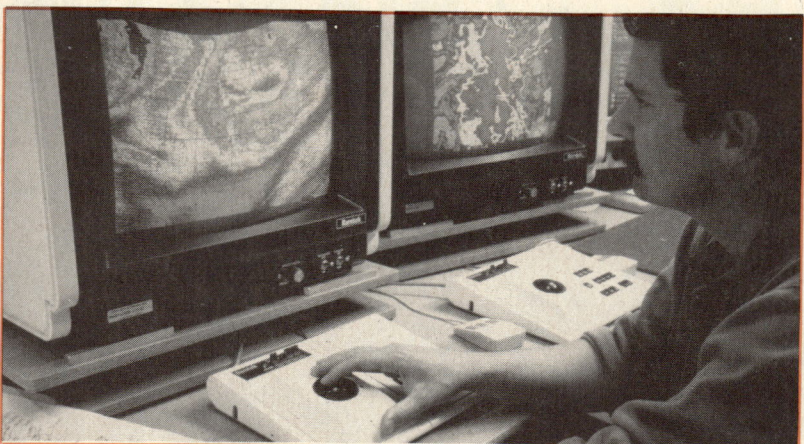

A meteorologist at work.

THINK IT THROUGH

Weather Reports

Part 1
Directions: Complete the sentences below. Sometimes two words are needed.

1. High winds on a cold day will increase the _____ _____.

2. If there is a tornado _____, weather conditions are just right for a tornado.

3. Hail is a form of _____.

4. A comparison of moisture in the air in the morning and at noon is called _____.

5. An average of temperature readings taken at different times during the day is called _____.

Part 2
Directions: Read each sentence. Write *F* if the sentence is a fact and *O* if it is an opinion.

_____ 1. Meteorologists are trained scientists.

_____ 2. Meteorologists are never right.

_____ 3. 65 mph is high wind velocity.

_____ 4. Barometric pressure of 30 is normal.

_____ 5. Hot, humid weather makes everyone uncomfortable.

_____ 6. Windchill factor is only in the mind.

_____ 7. Certain words in weather reports indicate change in weather.

ANOTHER LOOK

Directions: Write a prediction about tomorrow's weather. Then name a fact that caused you to make your prediction.

Your prediction: _____
_____
_____
_____
_____
_____

Fact that caused you to make prediction: _____
_____
_____
_____
_____
_____
_____
_____
_____
_____

VOCABULARY

barometer
an instrument that measures air pressure

barometric
having to do with a barometer

forecast
prediction about the weather

humidity
dampness; amount of moisture in the air

meteorologists
scientists who study weather

precipitation
water that falls to earth as hail, mist, rain, sleet, or snow

prediction
a statement about what may happen in the future

temperatures
degrees of heat or cold

velocity
speed

windchill factor
measures how much colder the wind makes the air feel

VOCABULARY PRACTICE

Part 1: Work with Weather Terms

Directions: Read the paragraph below. Then fill in the blanks with one of the words in **dark type**.

**barometer   velocity   temperatures
predict   meteorologists**

Before the invention of the _____ and other instruments, people used other means to study the weather. Often, they would _____ the weather based on the way the sky looked. For instance, the ancient Chinese believed that a halo was the sign of high wind _____ and rain. Modern _____ say that some of these old methods have a sound basis. For example, a red sky in the evening usually does mean pleasant _____ the next day.

Part 2: Using Words Correctly

Directions: Below are pairs of sentences. Only one sentence in each pair uses the underlined word correctly. Circle the letter of each sentence that is correct.

1. (a) After checking the barometer, Jim said that it might rain.
   (b) They measured the temperature using a barometer.

2. (a) The precipitation was clocked at 25 mph.
   (b) Precipitation in cold weather makes the roads icy.

3. (a) The humidity is low today, so older people should stay indoors.
   (b) Heat and high humidity can ruin a hairstyle.

4. (a) The famous meteorologist predicted the hurricane.
   (b) The famous meteorologist studied the planets.

WORD ATTACK

Root Review

This chapter is a review of the roots you have learned. Study the chart below and complete the exercise.

Root	Meaning	Example
tele	far off, distant	telephoto
phone, phono	voice, sound	gramophone, phonometer
gram, graph	written	telegram, autograph
photo	light	photograph
scope	to watch, to look at	telescope
bio	life	biometrics
meter	instrument that measures	taxometer
hydro	water	hydrology
logy	study of	sociology

PRACTICE

Directions: Match the words on the left with the definitions on the right.

____ 1. zoo*logy*

____ 2. *photo*meter

____ 3. micro*scope*

____ 4. bio*graphy*

____ 5. *hydro*plane

____ 6. *tele*pathy

(a) a speed boat that barely touches the *water*

(b) a device for *looking at* very small objects

(c) an *instrument that measures light* of the stars

(d) communicating thoughts with a person who is *far away*

(e) the *study of* animals

(f) a *writing* about a person's *life*

FOR FUN

Reading a Weather Map

Directions: This map appeared in a city newspaper. Study the key symbols that appear below. Then answer the questions that follow.

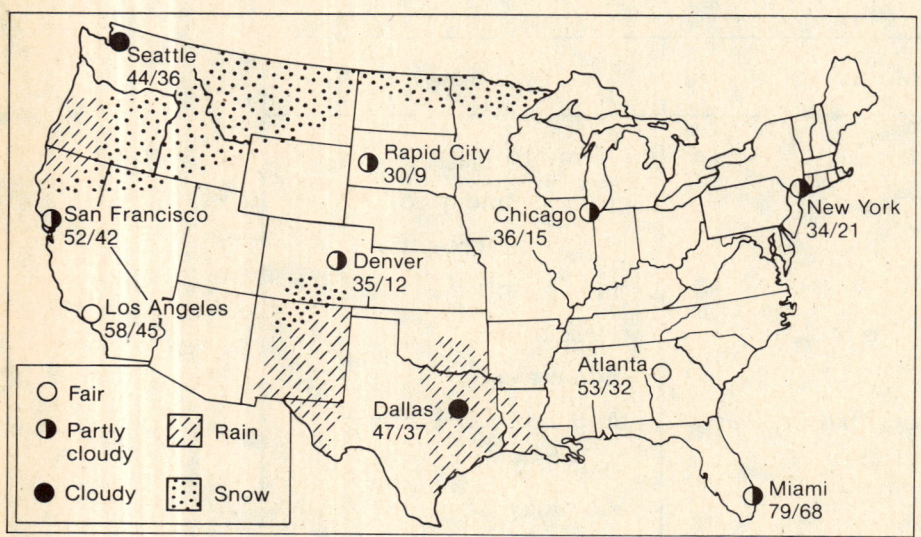

1. Look at the key at the bottom of the map. What does ◐ stand for? _____

2. What does ⊡ stand for? _____

3. Is rain predicted for Atlanta, Georgia? _____

4. What will be the high temperature in San Francisco? _____

5. What is the lowest temperature expected in New York? _____

6. How many of the cities shown have cloudy conditions? _____

7. Which city has the lowest temperature? _____

8. Which city has the highest temperature? _____

9. In how many cities is the lowest temperature above freezing (32 degrees)? _____

10. Based on the temperatures, in which season do you think this weather map was drawn? _____

12 Community Recycling

Minutes of special meeting, July 1, 1989
Sixth Street Block Club

Present: Donald Brown, Ellen Beavers, Frank Timmons, Lou Wing, Doris King, Fred James, and guest, Dan Jones.

The meeting was called to order by President Donald Brown. The guest speaker, Dan Jones, was introduced by the treasurer, Frank Timmons.

Mr. Jones is the coordinator of Tickstone Recycling Center. He encouraged our block club to take part in their recycling program. Ellen Beavers asked how the recycling program works. Mr. Jones said that community residents save old newspapers and empty bottles and cans. They bring these materials to the recycling center and get money in return. For instance, the center pays 2¢ for each pound of glass and 50¢ for each pound of aluminum cans. The center sends the materials back to factories where they are made into new products.

Lou Wing pointed out that this sounded like a lot of work for people in the community.

Mr. Jones agreed, but he argued that it was still a good idea. He explained that the city's landfills are overcrowded with garbage. If too much garbage is put into a landfill, poisons can seep into the ground and threaten the city's water supply. Also, landfills give off poisonous gases.

Fred James asked if it were true that poor communities have fewer recycling programs.

Mr. Jones said yes. In these areas, people tend to know less about recycling. Also, people with less money tend to buy cheaper products that don't last very long. As a result, more items are thrown away.

Mr. Brown asked the block club to support the recycling program and launch a community clean-up campaign.

Lou Wing offered a motion for the Sixth Street Block Club to join the Tickstone Recycling Center program.

The motion was passed by all present.

The meeting was adjourned.

Doris King
Secretary

Why is recycling necessary?

SKILL BUILD

Making a Hypothesis

Some Tickstone residents live near the landfill where the city's garbage is dumped. Over the years, these residents have been sick more often than people who live far from the landfill. Their hypothesis, or guess, is that living near the landfill affects their health. A **hypothesis** is a good guess based on the facts. It is an explanation of the facts.

We make hypotheses every day. For example, say that you came home and found that your front door had been opened and your television was missing. You would probably make the hypothesis that someone had broken into your home. This would be a good explanation of the facts.

Try forming a hypothesis from the statements below.

1. Eagles were once plentiful in the United States.
2. It used to be legal to hunt eagles.
3. Today, there are fewer eagles in the United States.

Hypothesis: _____

Did you say that hunters probably killed many of the eagles? That would be a logical guess.

Now try another one. Make a hypothesis from these statements.

1. At Major Supermarket, plastic grocery bags have always been used.
2. Recyclers believe that paper bags are better.
3. Recently, the market has started to use paper bags.

Hypothesis: _____

Did you say that an environmental group has put pressure on the market or that some of the workers are interested in recycling? Both of these would be good hypotheses.

Notice that you can make more than one hypothesis. Any hypothesis is valid as long as it explains the facts.

▼ POINT TO REMEMBER

A hypothesis is a good guess based on the facts. It is an explanation of the facts.

HYPOTHESIS PRACTICE

Directions: Read about each situation. Then write a hypothesis to explain it. Remember that there could be more than one hypothesis.

1. Old tires can be made into recycled oil and methane gas. But many car owners leave their used tires in vacant lots.

   Hypothesis: _____
   _____

2. The U.S. recycles only 12% to 15% of its glass containers, while Japan recycles 95% of its glass bottles.

   Hypothesis: _____
   _____

3. You hear that your friend Hilary has been taken to a hospital. You know that she is eight months pregnant.

   Hypothesis: _____
   _____

4. You have heard rumors that your company might close. One day, your boss calls everyone together and says he has something important to announce.

   Hypothesis: _____
   _____

5. You are driving on the highway, and you see a long line of cars ahead of you.

   Hypothesis: _____
   _____

ONE MORE STEP

Directions: Tell about a situation in your life that you don't understand. For instance, maybe your car doesn't start and you can't tell why, or maybe your oven won't heat and you don't know why. Then form a hypothesis that explains the situation.

Situation: _____
_____
_____
_____
_____
_____

Hypothesis: _____
_____
_____
_____
_____
_____

America's Trash Problem

Every year, Americans throw away enough writing paper to build a 12-foot wall from New York City to Los Angeles. We throw away enough glass bottles and jars every two weeks to fill a skyscraper. We **discard** enough aluminum to rebuild all of the commercial planes in the United States every three months.

Why shouldn't we just throw our trash away? Most garbage is dumped in **landfills**. But these landfills are quickly filling up, and they give off **toxic** gases. Another option is to **incinerate**, or burn, trash. When trash is burned, though, **toxins** that can cause serious health problems are released into the air.

Whether trash is dumped or burned, the cost of hauling and collecting it is high. In some cities, trash disposal costs as much as $100 a year per person. Tax dollars pay this cost.

What can we do to lessen these problems? Instead of throwing trash away, we can recycle some of it. To **recycle** means to use more than once. For example, empty beer cans may be sent to a factory to be recycled. The cans are smashed, remelted, and made into new cans. They are sent to another factory, filled with beer, and sold again. In a similar way, we can also recycle paper and glass.

Recycling costs less than dumping garbage in landfills or incinerating it. It also saves our natural **resources**, like forests, oil, and iron ore. For instance, when we recycle newspapers, we preserve the trees that would have been used to make the paper.

Another way to fight the trash problem is to use products that are **biodegradable**, or broken down by nature. If you bury paper in a landfill, it will break down over time and become part of the soil. Plastic, on the other hand, does not **decompose**. It remains intact for thousands of years. The only way to destroy it is to burn it, and burning plastic gives off toxic fumes. Some plastics now can be recycled, but the cost is very high.

Even in your personal life, you can help reduce the trash problem. Buy products you can reuse rather than products that you use once and throw out. When you have a choice, buy products that are paper or glass rather than plastic. At the supermarket, buy foods with no fancy packaging, since the paper and plastic packing will end up in your garbage. And of course, take your old cans, bottles, and paper to a recycling center. ■

Why is trash a problem in the United States today?

THINK IT THROUGH

Why Recycle?

Part 1
Directions: Use information from the reading to answer each question below.

1. Name two ways to dispose of trash:
   a. _____
   b. _____

2. Name two problems with landfills:
   a. _____
   b. _____

3. Name two natural resources:
   a. _____
   b. _____

4. Name two materials that can be recycled:
   a. _____
   b. _____

5. Name two ways that you can be a recycler:
   a. _____
   b. _____

Part 2
Directions: Answer each question below.

1. What do you think has caused the trash problem?
   _____
   _____

2. Why do you think people buy throw-away goods?
   _____
   _____

ANOTHER LOOK

Directions: Think of one way that you have seen resources abused in your community, such as trash in the streets or an overflowing landfill. Write a few sentences describing the problem. Then form a hypothesis to explain what you saw.

Resource abuse: _____
_____
_____
_____

Hypothesis: _____
_____
_____
_____

Now think of another instance of resource abuse and write a hypothesis.

Resource abuse: _____
_____
_____
_____

Hypothesis: _____
_____
_____
_____

VOCABULARY

biodegradable
able to be broken down by nature

decompose
to break down naturally

discard
throw away

incinerate
burn

landfill
garbage dump; a place where trash is buried

recycle
to use again

resource
a supply that can be used up

toxic
poisonous; harmful; deadly

toxin
a poison

VOCABULARY PRACTICE

Part 1: Use Recycling Terms

Directions: Complete each sentence below. Fill in the blanks with one of the words in **dark type**.

> discard   incinerate   toxic
> decompose   biodegradable   recycle
> resource   landfill

1. Sleeping pills can be _____.

2. They dumped garbage into the _____.

3. _____ your plastic shopping bags! Use them to store fruits and vegetables.

4. If you _____ that can of spray paint, it will get too hot and explode.

5. Since there is a limited supply of clean water, it is an important _____.

6. It's a good idea to _____ spoiled food.

7. Dead animals begin to _____ after several days.

8. Cloth and wood can be broken down by nature; they are _____.

Part 2: Match Words to Examples

Directions: Match each vocabulary word in the left column with the correct set of examples on the right.

___ 1. landfills   (a) forests, clean air, oil
___ 2. resources   (b) cyanide, arsenic
___ 3. toxins   (c) waste dumps

Part 3: Work with Recycling Words

Directions: Write a sentence using each word pair.

1. recycling—resources

   _____

2. biodegradable—decompose

   _____

WORD ATTACK

Review of Word Parts

In this book, you've learned a lot about word parts—prefixes, suffixes, and roots. Now it's time to review what you know.

If you like, look back at pages 31, 39, 47, 63, and 87 before completing the exercise that follows.

PRACTICE

Directions: Use what you know about word parts to find the meaning of each word below. Write a definition for the word, using a dictionary if you need one. Then write a sentence using the word. The first one is done for you.

	Word	Definition	Use in Sentence
1.	recycle	to use again	It is smart to recycle bottles.
2.	antiwar		
3.	nonreturnable		
4.	discard		
5.	immortal		
6.	preheat		
7.	psychology		
8.	biodegradable		
9.	misbehave		
10.	monogram		
11.	dehydrate		
12.	astronaut		
13.	thermal underwear		
14.	postnatal care		

FOR FUN

Recycler's Shopping List

The Wilson family has just joined a community recycling program. Cans, bottles, and newspapers are picked up weekly by a truck from the recycling center.

The Wilsons are studying a list of suggestions for shopping wisely. Study the list with them. Then help them decide which types of items they should purchase.

Shopping Tips
- Avoid plastic bottles and plastic containers
- Avoid one-use, throw-away products
- Choose appliances that have a long warranty and can be repaired
- Buy products that come in returnable containers, such as soda in glass bottles
- Buy products made of recycled material
- Avoid over-packaging
- Bring your own shopping bags when possible. Refuse extra bags
- Avoid fast-food restaurants that serve food in styrofoam containers

Now help the Wilson family shop wisely. Read their shopping list below. Write *yes* next to each item they should purchase and *no* next to each item they should not purchase.

_____ 1. Vitamins in glass bottles

_____ 2. Vitamins in plastic containers

_____ 3. Disposable diapers

_____ 4. Cloth diapers

_____ 5. Throw-away razors

_____ 6. Plastic picnic plates

_____ 7. TV with a one-year warranty

_____ 8. TV with a three-month warranty

_____ 9. Pop in returnable bottles

_____ 10. Greeting cards printed on recycled paper

_____ 11. Single cheese slices individually wrapped in plastic

_____ 12. Coffee in a styrofoam cup

Answer Key

1 An Unusual Teacher

Finding Details Practice
page 3

1. a. The story is about Maria James.
   b. She studied for the test.
   c. Her mother woke her at 9:00 the next morning.
   d. It took place in Maria's home.
   e. She dreamt that she had already taken it.
2. a. The parents are Jules and Marta Zimmer.
   b. The teachers' strike forced them to use their vacation time.
   c. The strike took place in September.
   d. They went to museums and parks.
   e. They spent a lot of time together.

One More Step
page 3
Answers will vary. Check your response with your instructor.

A Good Education?
page 5
Part 1
1. The U.S. government put out the report.
2. National test scores were higher in 1982.
3. Employers and colleges have complained about poor skills.
4. Few people are attracted to teaching because the pay is so low.
5. Parents can help their children by getting involved.

Part 2
1. No. The reading says that many people who hold diplomas have not learned what they should have in school.
2. Here are some possibilities: drugs, gangs, teen pregnancy.
3. Parents and teachers
4. They can help by passing laws that will help the schools.

Another Look
page 5
Answers will vary. Check your response with your instructor.

Vocabulary Practice
page 6
1. (c) diplomas
2. (c) opposite
3. (b) involvement
4. (d) salaries
5. (d) administrators
6. (b) national

Suffixes
page 7
1. teacher—2
2. spending—2
3. school—1
4. learner—2
5. testing—2
6. highest—2
7. slowly—2
8. commitment—3
9. study—2
10. math—1

School Ethics
page 8
Answers will vary. Check your response with your instructor.

2 Cora's New Home

Restating Practice
page 11
Part 1
1. (d)
2. (a)
3. (e)
4. (c)
5. (b)

Part 2
Answers will vary. Below are possible answers. Check your response with your instructor.
1. It costs a lot to buy a brand-new home.
2. Older houses may burn more easily.
3. The Tates took out a loan to buy their home.
4. The Rothmans would rather live in an apartment than a house.

One More Step
page 11
Answers will vary. Check your response with your instructor.

Who Pays for Housing?
page 13
Part 1
1. less
2. livable
3. repair

Part 2

Some possible restatements are listed below.

1. The federal government spent less money on housing during the 1980s and 1990s.
2. Instead, city and state governments had to pay for housing.
3. Many people lost their homes after the national government stopped providing money.
4. Different groups are working together to ease the housing crisis.

Another Look
page 13

Answers will vary. Check your response with your instructor.

Vocabulary Practice
page 14

Part 1
1. income
2. tenants
3. renovate
4. volunteers
5. community
6. Developers
7. mortgage payments
8. profit

Part 2
1. volunteer
2. profit
3. profit
4. volunteer

More Suffixes
page 15

1. a person who buys something
2. a person who rents
3. a person who acts
4. a person who accounts for people's money

Answers to sentences 1 and 2 will vary. Make sure that you used each word correctly.

Buying Property
page 16

1. (b)
2. (e)
3. (a)
4. (d)
5. (c)

3 A Farmer's Day

Summarizing Practice
page 19

Answers will vary, but your sentences should be similar to the examples that follow.
1. Some insects and animals that seem to be pests are actually helpful.
2. Grasshoppers are powerful, destructive insects.
3. Our dog Shepherd had a special knack for bringing the cows home.
4. Farmhouses differ from city dwellings in several ways.
5. The Brooklyn Bridge has supported car and foot traffic for over 100 years.

One More Step
page 19

Answers will vary. Check your response with your instructor.

How Did Farms Change?
page 21

1. False. Farms have changed greatly because of machines, government loans, and corporate farming.
2. False. Most farm work was done by hand.
3. False. The family is smaller than it was 100 years ago. Farmers no longer need many children to help with the work.
4. False. When food prices go down, there is less money to be made in farming, so fewer people will be farmers.
5. True. The trend is toward corporate farming.

Another Look
page 21

Answers will vary. Check your response with your instructor.

Vocabulary Practice
page 22

Part 1
1. fertilizer
2. debt
3. surplus
4. average
5. developer
6. corporate farm
7. acres
8. subsidies

Part 2
1. manage
2. develop
3. develop
4. manage

More Suffixes
page 23

1. without children
2. like a boy
3. full of events; busy
4. something that can be used

Getting Around
page 24
1. The scale of miles is in the lower left corner of the map.
2. Freeport is east of Pearl City.
3. He should go north.
4. They travel about 20 miles.
5. She travels about 26 miles.
6. It will be shorter if he takes Routes 73 to 20.

4 Mark Twain

Main Idea Practice
page 27
1. Main idea: Samuel Clemens chose the pen name Mark Twain with care.
2. Main idea: During his lifetime, Mark Twain was more popular as a speaker than as a writer.
3. Main idea: Mark Twain once insulted another speaker by accident.
4. Main idea: Tom is always pulling pranks on his friends and relatives.
5. Main idea: *The Adventures of Huckleberry Finn* is about a young boy, Huck Finn, and a runaway slave named Jim.

One More Step
page 27
Answers will vary. Check your response with your instructor.

What Caused the War?
page 29
Part 1
1. Jefferson Davis
2. slavery, or the slave system
3. Abraham Lincoln was president of the United States during the Civil War.
4. Emancipation Proclamation
5. No state could secede from the Union, and slavery was abolished by the Thirteenth Amendment.

Part 2
The numbers should be listed in this order: 5, 2, 1, 3, 4.

Another Look
page 29
Answers will vary. Check your response with your instructor.

Vocabulary Practice
page 30
Part 1
1. oppose
2. abolitionists
3. slavery
4. document
5. Emancipation Proclamation
6. Confederacy
7. Union
8. surrendered

Part 2
1. document
2. support
3. document
4. support

Prefixes
page 31
1. **inter**state: between states
2. **anti**nuclear: against the use of nuclear power
3. **mis**lead: to lead in the wrong direction; to deceive
4. **un**loved: not loved
5. **re**run: a show that is run again
6. **un**happy: not happy

Reading Maps
page 32
1. lighter
2. California, Oregon
3. Kentucky, Missouri, Delaware, and Maryland
4. Any five of these: Texas, Louisiana, Arkansas, Mississippi, Alabama, Georgia, Florida, Tennessee, South Carolina, North Carolina, Virginia
5. Five: Florida, Georgia, South Carolina, North Carolina, and Virginia

5 Rosa Parks

Inference Practice
page 35
Part 1
1. (b) You know this because Dr. King recalls how much money was given.
2. (c) You know this because everyone in the freedom movement carried toothbrushes in case they were taken to jail.

Part 2

Answers will vary. One possible answer is that the person is part of a boycott. Check your response with your instructor.

One More Step
page 35

Your inference should be similar to this: Dr. King thought that he had been too "patient," and he planned to protest.

What Are Civil Rights?
page 37
Part 1

1. You could have named any three of the following:
   the end of segregation on public transportation;
   the end of segregated schools and public facilities;
   removal of signs that read "Whites Only";
   voting rights (the Voting Rights Bill);
   equal employment opportunities (the Civil Rights Act).
2. No, the bill protects all peoples' right to vote.
3. No, the Civil Rights Act protects women *and* men of any color, race, religion, or nationality.

Part 2

Answers will vary. Here are some possible answers.
1. The Ku Klux Klan conducted lynchings and night raids.
2. One result of the civil rights movement was the Civil Rights Act, which protects job hunters from discrimination.
3. During "sit-ins," black and white people sat together.
4. The Voting Rights Act outlawed registration tests.

Another Look
page 37

Answers will vary. Check your response with your instructor.

Vocabulary Practice
page 38
Part 1

Civil rights have been won through much struggle. In the 1960s, people gathered in **protest** to stage **demonstrations** against segregation. The years from 1955 to 1965 marked a **decade** of civil rights activity. As a result, public **facilities** are now open to all races. All Americans have the right to sit in any bus seat or eat in any **restaurant**.

Part 2

You should have circled 3 and 5. Protests and demonstrations helped people get civil rights.

Part 3

Answers will vary, but your sentences should be similar to these.
1. People fought discrimination with boycotts.
2. The end of segregation was an important achievement.

Prefixes That Mean "Not"
page 39

You should have listed the letters in this order:
1. (c)   4. (d)
2. (e)   5. (b)
3. (a)   6. (f)

Win Your Rights!
page 40
1. (d)   5. (a)
2. (c)   6. (e)
3. (e)   7. (a)
4. (b)   8. (a)

6 An International Hero

Predicting Practice
page 43
Part 1

(a) Jack will take up a sport to improve his mental health.

Part 2

1. (a) Without Huntley, the team will lose its next game.
2. (c) Cragin will likely study harder to get a B average.

One More Step
page 43

Your prediction about the future of salaries in baseball should be similar to this: Salaries in baseball will continue to rise.

Puerto Rico: Some Facts
page 45

1. Caribbean
2. San Juan
3. Spanish
4. 3,670,000
5. Taino
6. 1493
7. 1898
8. 1952
9. citizens
10. warm
11. humid
12. rainy
13. sheep
14. cattle
15. pigs
16. poultry
17. coffee
18. sugarcane
19. tobacco
20. bananas

Another Look
page 45

Answers will vary. Check your response with your instructor.

Vocabulary Practice
page 46

Part 1
1. island
2. tropical
3. population
4. chemicals
5. Caribbean

Part 2
1. climate
2. territory
3. climate
4. territory

More Prefixes
page 47

1. e
2. f
3. g
4. b
5. h
6. a
7. d
8. c

What's the Score?
page 48

Year	H	HR	RBI	BA
1954	38	2	12	.257
1960	179	16	94	.314
1966	202	29	119	.316
Career Totals	3,000	240	1,305	.317

7 The Paycheck

Comparison and Contrast Practice
page 51

Part 1
1. comparison
2. contrast
3. comparison
4. contrast

Part 2
1. contrast
2. comparison
3. contrast
4. comparison

One More Step
page 51

Answers will vary. Check your response with your instructor.

Paycheck Deductions
page 53

Part 1
1. F
2. T
3. T
4. F
5. T

Part 2
1. (b)
2. (a)
3. (c)
4. (c)

Another Look
page 53

Answers will vary. Check your response with your instructor.

Vocabulary Practice
page 54

Part 1
1. union
2. net
3. Net income
4. deduction
5. insurance
6. social security
7. Gross
8. union

Part 2

For more than 100 years, U.S. citizens have had to pay **income tax**. Over the years, these taxes have helped pay for national defense, new roads, better schools, and aid to farmers. In 1935, the U.S. government started FICA, or **social security**. This program gives assistance to elderly and retired people. Both of these deductions are **involuntary**. Most **employees** must pay these taxes.

Word Families
page 55
Part 1

	Prefix	Suffix	Syllables
1.	—	ing	2
2.	un	ing	3
3.	—	er	2
4.	re	—	2
5.	un	able	4

Seeing Likenesses and Differences
page 56
Answers will vary, but the following are possible answers. Check your response with your instructor.

1. Both are places to work. / Most offices are in cities. Farms are in the country.
2. Both serve food. / Waiters are men. Waitresses are women.
3. Both are money. / Paychecks are for a specific person. Anyone can use cash.
4. Both are people. / Citizens have certain rights that foreigners don't.
5. Both are deducted from a paycheck. / Health plan is a voluntary deduction. Income tax is not.
6. Both are in a workplace. / The employer is in charge of the employee.
7. Both are changes in a paycheck. / The first is money taken out; the second is money added.
8. Both are countries. / Thailand is in the East. The United States is in the West.

8 Job Clinic

Cause-and-Effect Practice
page 59
Part 1
1. cause
2. cause
3. cause
4. effect
5. effect
6. effect
7. cause

Part 2
Answers will vary. Here are some possible answers.
1. Her boss will be worried.
2. Milton will quit.
3. Anita will feel pressured and unhappy.
4. Leonard will ask for a raise.

One More Step
page 59
Answers will vary. Check your response with your instructor.

Good Work Behavior
page 61
Part 1
1. F
2. F
3. F
4. T
5. T

Part 2
You should have checked sentences 2, 3, and 6.

Another Look
page 61
Answers will vary. Check your response with your instructor.

Vocabulary Practice
page 62
Part 1
1. dependable
2. accomplishment
3. Creative
4. behavior
5. courtesy
6. promptness
7. advancements
8. individual

Part 2
1. eagerness
2. environment
3. creative
4. behavior

Prefixes and Suffixes
page 63
Part 1

	Prefix	Main Word	Suffix
1.	non	smoke	ing
2.	mis	spell	ed
3.	un	like	able
4.	un	employ	ed
5.	dis	enchant	ed

Writing a Memo
page 64
Answers will vary. Below are possible answers. Check your response with your instructor.
1. mean, nasty
2. He may get angry and fire Kevin.
3. Mr. Carter, could I speak with you soon? My new work area is very cold and drafty, and I'm afraid I'll get sick. Would it be possible to move my desk back?

9 Meggie Talks About Goals

Sequence Practice
page 67

Part 1
You should have listed the pictures in this sequence: c, b, d, a.

Part 2
You should have circled the following signal words: *Later*, *After*, *Next*, *Since* and *Now*.

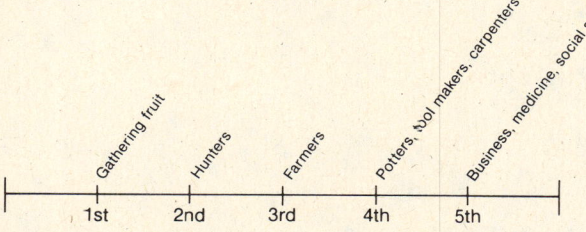

One More Step
page 67
Answers will vary. Check your response with your instructor.

Setting Goals
page 69
Part 1
1. career
2. public library
3. newspapers
4. role model
5. conferences

Part 2
1. information
2. cannot
3. can
4. do
5. an important step in reaching a goal

Another Look
page 69
Answers will vary. Check your response with your instructor.

Vocabulary Practice
page 70
Part 1
1. announcements
2. realistic
3. descriptions
4. obstacles
5. experts
6. occupation

Part 2
1. (b)
2. (d)
3. (i)
4. (h)
5. (c)
6. (j)
7. (e)
8. (g)
9. (a)
10. (f)

Roots
page 71
1. (c)
2. (e)
3. (b)
4. (d)
5. (a)

Picturing Your Ideal Job
page 72
Answers will vary. Make sure that you have written both a list of complaints and a list of statements about your ideal job.

10 Horoscopes

Finding Facts Practice
page 75
Part 1
1. NF
2. F
3. F
4. NF
5. F
6. NF
7. F
8. F

Part 2
You should have checked 2 and 4.

One More Step
page 75
Answers will vary. Check your response with your instructor.

Star Groups
page 77
Part 1
1. is not
2. stars
3. is not
4. twins
5. 88

Part 2
1. Answers will vary, but here are three possible facts:
   Constellations are groups of stars.
   There are 88 known constellations.
   Twelve constellations make up the zodiac.
2. Yes, they created star maps which are still used today.
3. They lacked scientific knowledge.
4. Answers will vary.
5. Answers will vary.

Another Look
page 77
Answers will vary. Check your response with your instructor.

Vocabulary Practice
page 78
Part 1
1. discredited
2. myths
3. constellations
4. ancient
5. zodiac

Part 2
1. (c)
2. (d)
3. (a)
4. (b)

Part 3
Answers will vary. Here are some possible sentences.
1. Astronomy is accepted by scientists, but astrology is not.
2. Myths were created to explain the constellations.

More Roots
page 79
1. (f)
2. (e)
3. (a)
4. (b)
5. (d)
6. (c)

Star Puzzle
page 80

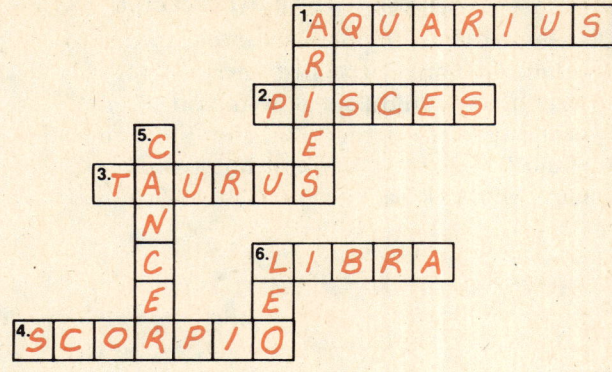

11 Diary of Janis Smith

Fact or Opinion Practice
page 83
Paragraph 1
1. F
2. O
3. F
4. O
5. O

Paragraph 2
1. F
2. F
3. F
4. O
5. O

One More Step
page 83
Answers will vary. Check your response with your instructor.

Weather Reports
page 85
Part 1
1. windchill factor
2. watch
3. precipitation
4. relative humidity
5. average temperature

Part 2
1. F
2. O
3. F
4. F
5. O
6. O
7. F

Another Look
page 85
Answers will vary. Check your response with your instructor.

Vocabulary Practice
page 86
Part 1

Before the invention of the **barometer** and other instruments, people used other means to study the weather. Often, they would **predict** the weather based on the way the sky looked. For instance, the ancient Chinese believed that a halo was the sign of high wind **velocity** and rain. Modern **meteorologists** say that some of these old methods have a sound basis. For example, a red sky in the evening usually does mean pleasant **temperatures** the next day.

Part 2
1. (a)
2. (b)
3. (b)
4. (a)

Root Review
page 87
1. (e)
2. (c)
3. (b)
4. (f)
5. (a)
6. (d)

Reading a Weather Map
page 88
1. partly cloudy
2. snow
3. no
4. 52
5. 21
6. two: Dallas and Seattle
7. Rapid City
8. Miami
9. five: Seattle, San Francisco, Los Angeles, Dallas, and Miami
10. winter

12 Community Recycling

Hypothesis Practice
page 91
Answers will vary, but here are some possible hypotheses:
1. Car owners do not know that tires can be recycled.
2. Japan has a more efficient recycling program.
3. Your friend is having a baby.
4. Your company is about to close.
5. There is road construction up ahead.

One More Step
page 91
Answers will vary. Check your response with your instructor.

Why Recycle?
page 93
Part 1
1. a. incinerating it
   b. dumping it in landfills
2. a. They give off poisonous gases.
   b. They are quickly filling up.
3. Any two of these: forests, oil, iron ore
4. Any two of these: paper, metal, glass, some plastics
5. Any two of these: buy reusable products; buy products with paper packaging; avoid products with too much packaging; recycle your cans, bottles, and newspapers

Part 2
1. Answers will vary. One possible answer is our lack of knowledge about recycling.
2. Answers will vary. One possible answer is that advertising causes people to buy throw-away goods; another is that disposable goods are often more convenient.

Another Look
page 93
Answers will vary. Check your response with your instructor.

Vocabulary Practice
page 94
Part 1
1. toxic
2. landfill
3. Recycle
4. incinerate
5. resource
6. discard
7. decompose
8. biodegradable

Part 2
1. (c)
2. (a)
3. (b)

Part 3
Answers will vary. Here are some possible sentences.
1. Recycling preserves our resources.
2. Objects that are biodegradable can decompose.

105

Review of Word Parts
page 95

	Definition	Use in Sentence
1.	to use again	It is smart to **recycle** bottles.
2.	against war	The **antiwar** group protested the draft.
3.	not returnable	Milk comes in **nonreturnable** plastic jugs.
4.	throw away	**Discard** the wrapper when you're finished eating.
5.	not mortal	The Greek gods were said to be **immortal**.
6.	heat (oven) before using	**Preheat** the oven to 350°.
7.	study of the mind	Use reverse **psychology** to make your kids do the cleaning.
8.	broken down by living things	Paper is **biodegradable**, but plastic is not.
9.	behave wrongly	Tell your children not to **misbehave**!
10.	writing that shows your initials or name	The sweater has a **monogram** with the initials *CB*.
11.	to dry out	Working all day in the sun can make a person **dehydrate**.
12.	person who travels through the stars	The **astronaut** boarded the spaceship.
13.	underwear that keeps you warm	Wear **thermal underwear** in winter.
14.	medical care after birth	A baby needs good **postnatal** care.

Recycler's Shopping List
page 96

1. yes — Avoid plastic bottles and containers; buy glass instead.
2. no — Avoid plastic bottles and containers.
3. no — Avoid throw-away products.
4. yes — Avoid throw-away products; buy reusable products instead.
5. no — Avoid throw-away products.
6. no — Avoid throw-away products.
7. yes — Choose appliances with long warranties.
8. no — Avoid appliances with short warranties.
9. yes — Buy products that come in returnable containers.
10. yes — Buy products made of recycled material.
11. no — Avoid over-packaging.
12. no — Avoid food served in styrofoam containers.